THE YOUNG OXFORD BOOK OF
FOOTBALL STORIES

THE YOUNG
OXFORD BOOK OF
FOOTBALL
STORIES

JAMES RIORDAN

Oxford University Press
Oxford   New York   Toronto

Oxford University Press, Great Clarendon Street, Oxford OX2 6DP

Oxford New York
Athens Auckland Bangkok Bogota Buenos Aires Calcutta
Cape Town Chennai Dar es Salaam Delhi Florence Hong Kong Istanbul
Karachi Kuala Lumpur Madrid Melbourne Mexico City Mumbai
Nairobi Paris São Paulo Singapore Taipei Tokyo Toronto Warsaw

and associated companies in
Berlin Ibadan

Oxford is a trade mark of Oxford University Press

This selection and arrangement © James Riordan 1998

The author has asserted his moral right to be
known as the author of the work.

First published 1998

British Library Cataloguing in Publication Data
Data available

Cover image supplied by Allsport,
photographed by Howard Boylan

ISBN 0 19 274180 2 (paperback)
ISBN 0 19 274179 9 (hardback)

Printed in Great Britain by Biddles Ltd, Guildford and King's Lynn

*To Tania and Marie, Sean and Perry,
and all long-suffering Pompey fans*

Contents

CONTENTS

Foreword

This is truly an excellent collection of football stories, covering the full range of emotions that everybody concerned with the game goes through during their lives. Whether you are a player or a fan, you can relate to this publication.

During the course of reading the book, I have found myself laughing at many of the particularly funny tales. However, the humorous aspects of the book are added to with many more serious stories which relate to a number of widely varying issues.

With football playing such an important role in the lives of youngsters away from school, I think it is tremendous that the game can also hold a key role in their wider personal development.

It is often said that youngsters learn more when they are especially interested in a subject. As the popularity of football continues to grow and grow, I am sure that this book will not only be enjoyed by everyone who reads it, but will also help with their education.

Enjoy the read.

Glenn Hoddle

Introduction

'Some people say football's a matter of life and death. That's ridiculous. It's far more important than that!'

Bill Shankly may have expressed his devotion to football a mite colourfully; but fans know what he meant. Those who care about football, from backyard to playground, from local park to stadium, are united by a love of something that is, for them, more than a game.

I've spent a fortune on football, following my team around the country, from top to bottom of the football leagues, up again, then down again, for over half a century. All our contributors are just as barmy as me in my support of Portsmouth—Michael Rosen of Arsenal, Robert Swindells of Bradford City, Celia Warren of Aston Villa, Michael Parkinson of Barnsley, Matt Simpson of Liverpool.

Most would gladly swap their writing for football skills. All played at one time, or still play now; they couldn't write so passionately about it otherwise. It was the novelist Albert Camus who once said he learned more from playing in goal for Algeria than he ever did from writing.

Mind you, Barry Hines (our hero!) made it to Barnsley Juniors and once played for the England Under-18s (they lost 0–3 to Scotland). And I once played a season for Moscow Spartak Reserves! Brian Glanville and Michael Parkinson did the next best thing by becoming football journalists.

Football can be a serious business. Tragically, for thousands of people it truly has been a matter of life or death—those burned to death in the terrible fire during a match at Bradford, those crushed to death at Heysel, Sheffield, and elsewhere. Joanna White remembers them in her moving poem-tribute to the Liverpool fans who died at Hillsborough in April 1989. *The Match of Death* is based on a true incident from World War II. And all fans will recognize the crowd violence described in the story by Robert Swindells.

Yet football can also bring hope and humour. It enables us to dream the impossible, as Michael Rosen shows with his fantasy team that plays in the Cup Final.

These and other stories and poems in this book are chosen to entertain. But more than that: they are meant to inspire, to make you laugh (and maybe cry), to fuel the dreams of all who truly love the game of football.

James Riordan

Going Up

ROBERT SWINDELLS

It was going to be the most exciting day of my life when Barfax Town played Lincoln City away in the last game of the season. If we won, Barfax would be promoted to the First Division for the first time since my dad was a kid. The whole town buzzed with it for a fortnight. You could feel the tension, just walking through the streets.

We had our tickets and seats on the coach. Dad and me, I mean. We never went to away matches but we were off to this one, no danger. Part-time supporters Dale always calls us, but it's not that. Dad works Saturday mornings so it's impossible for him to get away in time. He'd got special permission this time though, like a lot of other guys in Barfax.

Dale's my brother. He's a red-hot Town supporter. Goes to every match, but not with Dad and me. He's sixteen and part of the Ointment. The Ointment are the Barfax headbangers, feared by every club in the land according to him. Dad reckons they're a bunch of tossers and Dale should kick 'em into touch but he won't. Dead loyal to Lud, see? Lud Hudson, leader of the Ointment and cock of the Barfax Kop.

Was, I should say. *Was* loyal, till all that stuff went

down at Lincoln. A right mess, that was. Total
bummer. If you're not doing anything special I'll tell
you all about it.

First thing was, Dad lost his half day off. Big job
came in at work and that was that. 'Sorry, Tel,' he
goes. 'Can't be helped.'

My name's Terry but everybody calls me Tel. And
yes I *know* I should've said, 'Ah well, it's only a game,'
but I didn't. I went ballistic instead. Well, this was
Thursday, right? *Two flipping days* before the match,
and I'd been building up to it for a fortnight. 'S'not
fair,' I screeched. 'Everyone else is off, why not me?
Our Dale's going.'

And that's when I got this brilliant idea. I could go
with Dale, couldn't I? I eyeballed Dad through my
tears. 'Why can't *Dale* take me—he's my brother, isn't
he?' You could see he wasn't keen. Dad, I mean. He
sighed, pulled a face.

'Our Dale . . . he's not *reliable*, Tel. It's those
headbangers he knocks around with. I wouldn't feel
easy in my mind . . .'

Easy in your mind? Wow, did I let rip. What about
my mind? What about I've been looking forward to this
match for *two weeks*? Why should *I* stay home while all
my mates're there, shouting for the Town? They'll
show off, Monday. Laugh at me. I won't dare show my
face at school.

And he gave in. Against his better judgement, he
said, but I didn't care. I was over the moon.

Our Dale wasn't. He went ape-shape. '*Tel?*' he yelps
when Dad mentions it. 'Drag our *Tel* along? You're
joking. My mates. Lud . . . I'll be a laughing stock,
Dad. They'll *crucify* me.'

Poor old Dad. Not only was he missing the match
himself, he was getting all this grief from the two of us
as well. Don't think I'll have any kids when *I* grow up.
Anyway, he lays into our Dale, tells him at sixteen it's
time he started taking a bit of responsibility and all

that, and in the end the big plonker agrees to take me. No choice really.

So. The big day rolled round at last, and at half eleven there I was in my Town scarf and cap, trotting at my brother's heels towards the coach park. He was going fast on purpose but I wasn't bothered. I'd have stuck with him somehow if he'd been Lynford flipping *Christie*. The road was crammed with folk in scarves and caps, all heading the same way. I bet most of 'em had never been to a match before in their lives.

You should've seen the coach park. Talk about seething. There must've been at least twelve coaches, and that's not counting all the people who were going by train or car. Dale heads straight for the Ointment coach. They don't have their own, I don't mean that, but they must've planned in advance to take one over because there they were in a mob by the door, shouting and laughing, stopping other folk from getting near. I don't suppose many people fancied travelling with them anyway.

'Hey up, Dale—started a day nursery, have you?' A great husky guy in black, studded leather looks from Dale to me and back to Dale.

My brother grins, sheepishly. 'Naw, just minding our Tel for the day. You know how it is.'

'You mean . . . Tel here's travelling with *us*?'

'Well, yeah, just this once. My old man . . .'

'Sod your old man. What if . . . ?'

'Hey, mind your language, Lud. I'll just have to . . . you know . . . stay out of it if it happens, that's all.'

'Stay *out* of it?' He scowled at my brother. Others were chuckling, nudging one another. I wished Dad was with us. 'Now you listen here, my son. You stay out today, you're *out*, geddit? Ointment don't *choose* when to rumble. Ointment's there for its mates, for the *Town*, see? Town pride, is what it's all about. You think about that all the way down, son, 'cause there ain't no *nannies* in the Ointment.'

He was great, that Lud. I mean, I *know* he was a thug, but you should've seen how he controlled those headbangers. They *worshipped* him. Nobody else could've done it.

It was terrific, that coach ride. See—to really enjoy a match there's got to be atmosphere, and those guys really knew how to build atmosphere. It was the jokes and the songs, especially the songs. What they did was, they started yelling for the kids in various parts of the bus to give them a song. You know—*back seat back seat sing us a song, back seat—sing us a song.* The kids on the back seat would sing a song, then it'd be, *front end front end sing us a song*—and so on. Just after Doncaster we ran over a dog, and like a flash they crowded up to the back window going, *dead dog dead dog sing us a song*—horrible I know, but magic too. I've never felt so fired up in my life.

We got to Lincoln just after one. The police were waiting to escort the Town fans, but Lud knew an alleyway and the Ointment slipped into it. Dale had ignored me on the coach and he ignored me now. I had to run to keep up as they negotiated the alley and headed for a pub they knew opposite the ground.

I'd never been in a pub. I didn't know kids could. I plucked at Dale's sleeve. 'I can't go in there. I don't want to.'

'Shut it, kid. You're with me, you go where I go. Come on.'

The place was packed. Smoky. They barged in, shouting and swearing, intimidating customers into making room for them. Nobody took any notice of me, it was like I wasn't there. All these bodies jostling, shoving me around. I couldn't see over them. It was taking me all my time to keep from falling. I was sweating like a pig and the smell of the place made me feel sick.

After a bit they found some seats—I think people left to get away from us—and Dale put me on a bench between two of the guys. He'd got me a Coke and some crisps. I thought, this is better. It's going to be all right now. They were talking about the match. Next season in the first division. Cheering and laughing, slurping pints. Dale had given over telling them to mind their language. I sat there and tried to be part of the Ointment.

It might have been OK if a crowd of Lincoln fans hadn't showed up. Twenty-past two and in they came in their colours, roaring. They knew we were there, and the Ointment had been expecting them. They leapt up, overturning chairs, knocking glasses and beermats on the floor, surging towards their challengers. In a second I went from being crammed in to having the whole bench to myself. I didn't know what I was supposed to do. *You're with me—you go where I go.* Was I meant to join the fight?

It *was* a fight, over there by the door. A terrible fight. Crashing and yelling and the sound of things breaking. The customers had fled out the back. There was just the fight, and a guy behind the bar on the phone, and me. I couldn't move. I sat there wishing I'd stayed home. I didn't care about the match any more, I just wanted to be somewhere familiar. Somewhere safe.

There was a noise, over the noise of fighting. Sirens. The Ointment and the Lincoln lads crammed the doorway, struggling to get out of the pub while continuing to knock hell out of one another. I looked for Dale but couldn't see him. He'd forgotten me. I was alone in a city I didn't know. A city full of enemies.

Suddenly the pub was empty. A guy charged over a sea of broken glass, aimed a kick at a youth in the doorway and the pair of them swayed snarling out of sight. I slipped off the bench and ran to the door, yelling for my brother. Two police cars stood at the kerb, blue lights flashing. The fight was a few metres away down the street. A woman somewhere screamed.

Dogs came out of a white van. Police dogs on leads, pulling their handlers towards the battle. The fighters broke and ran, all except one who stood bent over, blood pouring from between the fingers he'd clamped to his face. It wasn't Dale. I started in the direction the fight had gone because I didn't know what else to do. I had my ticket, but I couldn't remember where the coaches were picking us up after. How could I watch a soccer match, knowing I was lost a hundred miles from home?

It was then I heard my name. 'Terry? What're you doing here? Where's your dad?' I turned, weak with relief. It was Popo, Dad's mate, with Danny his son, same age as me.

I shook my head. 'Dad couldn't come. Work. I'm with Dale, but he's . . .' I gestured towards the dog-handlers. 'He's somewhere, fighting.'

'Oh, I see. Oh dear. Well, you'd better come with us, I think. Never know when Dale might . . . got a ticket, have you?'

'Yes.' I got it out, showed him. I'd never been so pleased to see anyone in my life.

He nodded, smiled. 'Come on then. We'll see Dale inside, I expect.'

We didn't though. Popo sat me and Danny on a rail so we could see over people's heads, and all through the match I kept looking round for my brother, except the last ten minutes when it got too nail-biting and I forgot. They were torture, those last ten minutes. We seemed to be heading for a goalless draw—missing out on promotion by two rotten points—when a Lincoln player fouled Billy Watson and the ref awarded Town a free kick just outside the box. Watson took it himself and it was a beauty, swerving round the end of their wall and ricocheting off the underside of the bar into the top right hand corner of the net. Half a centimetre higher and it'd have bounced out. You should've heard us roar. You probably *did*—it's only a hundred miles after all. Anyway there were ten minutes left and they chucked everything at us. I'm not kidding—even their *goalie* had a shot. Well, they'd nothing to lose and everything to gain, but it was no use. Our lads hung on and that's how we went up.

Popo drove me home. Danny and I clamped our scarves in the windows so they flapped in the slipstream all the way up the A1.

That's the good news. The bad news is that Dale didn't make it home that night, and poor Lud didn't make it at all. Somebody stabbed him and he died in hospital without ever knowing the result of the match. None of the Ointment saw the game. By the time Watson swerved us into Division One they were all down the police station being charged. It was Sunday lunchtime when our Dale turned up. He'd come by train, and he was breathing funny owing to bruised ribs. Dad had intended giving him hell for leaving me, but he looked so rough he let him stagger off to bed.

Monday teatime we're all in the front room watching telly. Town on an open top bus getting a civic reception, but when the chairman comes on our Dale gets up and leaves the room because he knows what he's going to say. Naturally he starts by regretting Lud's tragic death, but then he says, 'Those youths who brawled on the streets of Lincoln last Saturday are not our supporters. They have no share in our triumph and are not welcome on our terraces. We are a First Division club with First Division fans. There is no place in our ranks for scum.'

A bit later on I go up to the toilet and pass Dale on the landing and he's been crying. 'Have I heck,' he says when I mention it, but he has. He's had the telly on in his room and heard the whole thing. Just can't admit it to his little sister, that's all.

Anyway, all this was last season. *This* season he's a different guy. He goes to every match same as before, only he doesn't stand with the Ointment. He doesn't stand with me and Dad either, but that's all right. He's *grown*, see? Just like Barfax Town.

Dad

In memory of those who died at Hillsborough, April 1989

Is it Saturday yet, Dad?
Have you got the tickets, Dad?
Are we going by train, Dad?
Will it be a good game, Dad?
Is it far to walk now, Dad?
Can you buy me a scarf, Dad?
Aren't there lots of people, Dad?
Can we go down to the front, Dad?
I am so very crushed, Dad!
I can hardly see, Dad!
I can't breathe, Dad!
Dad! . . . Dad! . . . Dad! . . .

Joanna White

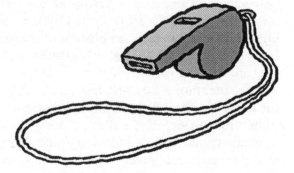

Clakker May

MICHAEL PARKINSON

I suspect that Clakker May would be regarded as a classic example by those people who reckon all goalkeepers are born crazy. You'd never suspect there was anything wrong by looking at him. He was a tall, stringy, quiet youth who lived with his parents and ten brothers and sisters in a council house near the pit gates. He became our goalkeeper quite by chance. One day we were a man short, and Len, our trainer, asked Clakker to play in goal. The result was a revelation. It wasn't so much when he donned the jersey he changed in his attitude towards his team-mates, it was simply that he believed that the rules of the game related to everyone except himself.

We became aware of his quirk the first time he touched the ball. He left his goal line to meet a hard, high cross, caught the ball cleanly, shaped to clear downfield, and then, for no apparent reason, spun round and fled to the back of the net. This move dumbfounded players, officials and spectators alike. As we stood gaping, Clakker ran from the back of the net and booted the ball over the halfway line. Nobody moved as it bounced aimlessly towards the opposite goal and then the referee broke the silence by blowing on his whistle and pointing to the centre spot. This appeared to upset Clakker.

'What's tha' playin' at?' he asked the referee.

'I was just about to ask thee same question,' said the referee.

By this time Len had run on to the field.

'What the bl— hell . . .' he began.

'Nay, Len. Tha' see I caught this ball and then I looks up and I saw this big centre forrard coming at me and I thought, "B—r this lot", so I got out of his way,' Clakker explained.

'Tha' ran into t'bl— net wi' t'ball and tha' scoored,' Len shouted.

'Scoored,' said Clakker, incredulously.

'Scoored,' said Len, emphatically.

Clakker shook his head. Len tried to keep calm. 'Look, lad,' he said, putting his arm round Clakker's shoulders. 'I know it's thi' first game and all that, but tha' must get one thing straight. When tha' catches t'ball gi' it some clog downfield. Whatever tha' does don't run into t'net.'

Clakker nodded.

But it made little difference. In the next twenty minutes Clakker ran into the net thirteen times and we were losing 14–2. At this point the referee intervened. He called us all together and said: 'Na' look, lads, this is making a mock of a great game. If it goes on like this t'scoor will be in t'hundreds and I'll have to mek a report to t'League Management Committee and there'll be hell to pay.' We all nodded in agreement. The referee thought a bit and then said: 'What we'll do is amend t'rules. If Clakker runs into t'back of t'net in future it won't count as a goal, allus providin' he caught t'ball on t'right side of t'line in t'first place.'

Everyone agreed and play continued with this extraordinary amendment to the rules. At the final whistle we had lost fifteen to five and Clakker had shown that apart from his eccentric interpretation of the rules he was a remarkably good goalkeeper. Nobody said much after the game. It seemed useless to ask Clakker what went wrong because all of us agreed that like all goalkeepers he was a bit screwy. Our theory was confirmed by Clakker's old man, who when told of his son's extraordinary behaviour simply shook his head and said, 'He allus was a bit potty.'

But that was not the end of Clakker's career, not quite. He was picked for the next game because we didn't want to hurt him too much. Len, the trainer, called us together on the night before the game and explained how we might curb Clakker's madness. His plan was that the defenders should close in behind Clakker whenever he went out for a ball and bar his way into the net. Any resistance from Clakker should be firmly dealt with and if possible the ball taken from him and cleared upfield. In case Clakker should break through his own rearguard Len had taken the precaution of hiding the nets. His theory was that provided Clakker ran into goal, but straight out again, the referee would be unable to decide what had happened.

The reports of our last game had attracted a large crowd to the ground for Clakker's second appearance. All his family were present to see if it was true what people were saying about Clakker's extraordinary behaviour.

Things worked quite well for a time. Every time Clakker caught the ball we fell in around him and urged him away from his goal. Once he escaped us and nipped into goal, but he had the sense to escape immediately around the goalpost and clear downfield. The referee looked puzzled for a minute and gave Clakker a peculiar look, but did not give a goal because he could not believe what he thought he saw. We were leading two goals to nil with five minutes of the first half left when Clakker gave the game away. Overconfident at having duped the referee once before, he ran over his own goal line with the ball. His plan came to grief when he collided with the iron stanchion at the back of the goal. As he staggered drunkenly against the support the referee blew for a goal and gave Clakker the sort of look that meant all was now revealed.

When half-time came none of us could look forward to the next forty-five minutes with any optimism. Len came on the field and beckoned myself and the centre half to one side. 'Na' look, lads, we've got to do something about yon Clakker,' he said. 'I've thought about playing him out of goal, but that's too dangerous. I can't just take him off because yon referee wouldn't allow it. So there's only one thing we can do.' He paused and looked at both of us.

'What's that?' I asked.

'Fix him,' said Len.

'Fix him?' I said.

Len nodded. 'When you get a chance, and as soon as you can, clobber him. I don't want him to get up, either,' said Len.

The centre half was smiling.

'Look,' I said to him, 'we can't clobber our own team-mate. It's not done.'

He looked at me pityingly. 'Leave it to me,' he said. 'I've fixed nicer people than Clakker.'

It took two minutes of the second half for Clakker to get fixed. There was a scrimmage in our goalmouth and when the dust had cleared Clakker lay prostrate on his goal line. Len came running on to the field, trying to look concerned. The centre half was trying hard to look innocent. Clakker's father had drifted over to the scene and was looking down at his son's body. 'He's better like that,' he said.

Len said to him, 'Tek your Clakker home and don't let him out till t'game's finished.'

Clakker's old man nodded and signalled to some of his sons to pick Clakker up. The last we saw of them they were carrying Clakker out of the field and home. We did quite well without him and managed to win. Afterwards in the dressing room some of the lads were wondering how Clakker became injured. Len said: 'Tha' nivver can tell wi' goalkeepers. It's quite likely he laid himself out.'

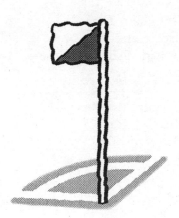

A Perfect Match

We met in Nottingham Forest,
  My sweet Airdrie and I.
She smiled and said, 'Alloa!' to me—
  Oh, never say goodbye!

I asked her, 'Is your Motherwell?'
  And she replied, 'I fear
She's got the Academicals
  From drinking too much beer.'

We sat down on a Meadowbank
  And of my love I spoke.
'Queen of the South,' I said to her,
  'My fires of love you Stoke!'

We went to Sheffield, Wednesday.
  Our Hearts were one. Said she:
'Let's wed in Accrington, Stanley,
  Then we'll United be.'

The ring was Stirling silver,
  Our friends, Forfar and wide,
A motley Crewe, all gathered there
  And fought to kiss the bride.

The best man had an awful lisp.
  'Come Raith your glatheth up,'
He said, and each man raised on high
  His Coca-Cola cup.

The honeymoon was spent abroad:
  We flew out east by Ayr,
And found the far-off Orient
  Partick-ularly fair.

We're home, in our own Villa now,
  (The Walsall painted grey)
And on our Chesterfield we sit
  And watch Match of the Day.

Pam Gidney

Even Stevens FC

MICHAEL ROSEN

Wayne Travis was football mad. So were most of his friends. Every day after school, they played 23-a-side football in the space round by the dustbins. No ref. One goal.

Wayne's ambition was to be a professional footballer. Every day he watched his *Goals of the Century* video and imagined being on television.

Wayne's other ambition was to perfect the famous Hedley Carlton Triple-Bounce Goal, as described to him by his grandad:

'I shall never forget that goal. It wasn't just the swerve; it wasn't just the speed; each bounce zigzagged across the pitch as if the ball had a life of its own.'

Wayne decided to have a go. His foot swerved as it approached the ball, then spun back the other way. At the same time it flipped up under the ball.

The result was amazing. The ball flew like a rocket towards Shaheed. It dipped, bounced, swerved off towards Roger and Harry. It bounced again and swerved back towards the two Shonas.

It bounced again and headed for Maxine and Lara.

Then it hurtled into the goal, hitting the wall with a thunderous wham.

16

From then on, Wayne practised the foot move whenever he could. Under the table, on the bus, at breakfast . . . swerve, spin-back, flip-up; swerve, spin-back, flip-up.

Wayne wasn't the only one in his family who liked football. On Saturday mornings Wayne's dad played for a team called Even Stevens.

Everyone in the team lived in Shakespeare Street. It was called Even Stevens because all the players lived in houses or flats with even numbers. They played their matches on the Astroturf behind the Mammoth Hypermarket.

EVEN STEVENS FC
Team Notes
(nicknames in brackets)

Erkan Hussein, 21. Leather worker. Excellent right foot, terrible left. Mother works at Tesco. (*Tesco*)

Harry Postlethwaite, 52. Bus driver. Terrible right foot, terrible left foot. Says he knew Sir Stanley Matthews. (*Stan*)

Darren Stewart, 13. School kid. Brilliant all-rounder. Only one eye. (*Nelson*)

Chuck Bradley, 35. Unemployed. Ex-American football player. (*Superbowl*)

Moira Stewart, 41. Darren's mum, ex-Scotland ladies team. (*Jock*)

Satoshi Watanabe, 20. Student. Broke Tokyo record for spinning a basketball on one finger. (*Guinness*)

Solly Rosenberg, 68. Once captained United London Jewish Boys clubs tour of Wales. (*Taffy*)

Linton Harper, 19. Computer salesman. Rap artist, team kit style consultant. Wikkid! (*Mr Kool*)

Linford Harper, 21. Linton's older brother. Bosses him around something shocking. (*Bossman*)

Nigel Fiddle, 18. Shoe shop assistant. Awful player, but can get football boots dead cheap. (*Start-rite*)

Rodney Travis, 38. Wayne's dad. Bad back, bad right knee, bad shoulder, bad neck. Part-time postman. (*Pat*)

Salvatore Delgado, 16. Claims to be grandson of reserve team member in 1970 world-cup winning Brazil squad. (*Pelé*)

Donna Louis, 16. Ex-spectator of Linton. Now plays in own right. (*Mrs Kool*)

One Friday night in September, Erkan called round to see Wayne's dad.

'Guess what, Pat, we're eligible for the FA Cup. The draw's just come through and we're up against Wealdstone next Saturday!'

'Wealdstone?' said Wayne's dad. 'But they're a really brilliant side, with ex-professionals. We'll be smashed.'

Erkan wasn't put off. He told all the members of the team the good news. But there were a few problems.

For one thing, Nigel Fiddle was in Latvia buying a stock of cheap shoes, so he wouldn't be able to play. For another, Wayne's dad now had a bad left knee, so he wouldn't be able to play either.

Undaunted, that Saturday Erkan led Even Stevens FC out to play Wealdstone on the Astroturf behind the Mammoth Hypermarket.

And in that team was young Wayne Travis.

For everyone in Shakespeare Street it was a huge thrill, but no one else took much notice, except for a woman from the local radio station who happened to be passing.

'Wealdstone's attack has been kept at bay by some extraordinary long-ball bouncing-passes by young Wayne Travis. They've just conceded a penalty in the eighty-ninth minute. 13-year-old Darren Stewart is taking the kick. He runs up . . . It's a goal! And there's the final whistle! Wealdstone have been beaten in the first qualifying round of the FA Cup!'

It turned out to be the scoop of the year for local radio.

Back in the dressing room (Moira Stewart's front room) Darren explained, 'The goalie was watching my face and not the ball. So I leered at him with my false eye and he went the wrong way.'

The next day, Wayne and the rest of the team tuned in to the local radio to hear the draw for the next round:

'. . . versus Hendon. Bishop Auckland versus Corinthian Casuals. Cartilege United versus Even Stevens. Pinner versus . . .'

'Yeees!' yelled Darren. 'Cartilege United! Didn't we beat them 4-nil only a few months back?'

Meanwhile, in a garden shed somewhere in Enfield, Cartilege United were not so happy . . .

'Oh no, Even Stevens. That really does it.'

'Sorry, I can't make September 28th. I've got to mow the lawn.'

'My brother's giving me a hair cut that day.'

'I've got to take the mower over to Uncle Bill's.'

'Yeah, me too, Dad.'

And so Even Stevens didn't have to play anyone at all in the next round of the FA Cup!

Successfully through the qualifying rounds, their next challenge was to play the non-league professionals. They were drawn away against the powerful Telford United. As the *Hackney Mercury* put it (in his 'On the Ball' column by Chris Hack):

Young Wayne Travis is on top of the world. Just 9 years old, he's in the country's greatest football tournament.

'It's brill,' states Wayne from his home in Shakespeare Street. 'His mum would've been proud of him,' adds Dad Rodney (38) part-time postman and widower.

And what of the amazing long-ball triple-bouncing passes we saw in the game?

'Just a fluke,' says fair-haired Wayne. 'I don't want to make too much of it.'

But it's certainly a RED LETTER day for Postman Dad!!!

When the big day came, Wayne's dad's knees were still playing up and Nigel was still in Latvia (or was it Poland?). So Wayne was in the team.

On the coach to Telford, Erkan dished out advice.

'I want commitment. Hard tackling in mid-field, early ball to Jock and Nelson up front. Zigzag (Wayne now had his own nickname, thanks to the Hedley Carlton Triple-Bounce), I want you to cover Taffy when he gets tired and only use that tricky long-ball bounce-pass when there's space down the middle.'

On the way to the game, the team sang songs in their coach:

> 'Even Stevens is the name,
> We're the best in the game,
> We're the best in the west,
> We're the best of the rest.'

On the way back from Telford . . .

'I haven't seen a match like that since the 1953 cup final when Stanley Matthews beat Bolton Wanderers single-handed.'

'Zigzag's passing was amazing.'

'But who got the winning touchdown, guys?'

'We call it a goal, Superbowl.'

By the time the coach got back to Hackney, the crowds were out to welcome them.

'There's only one Wayne Travis,
There's only one Wayne Travis.'

'Su-per, super bowl,
Su-per, super bowl.'

'Mrs Kool
Mrs Kool,
Mrs, Mrs Kool,
She's got long hair,
And she don't care,
Mrs, Mrs Kool.'

Next day, the draw for the first round of the FA Cup took place on TV.

'Even Stevens versus Blackpool . . .'

Old Harry Postlethwaite couldn't believe his ears.

'I don't believe it! That's Stanley Matthews's old team. When we beat . . .'

'Bolton Wanderers single-handed in the 1953 cup final!' chorused his family.

'Will I get to play?' wondered Wayne.

He needn't have worried.

'We need you, Zigzag,' shouted Satoshi. 'No one can read your game.'

The Astroturf at the back of the Mammoth Hypermarket had never known anything like it. The car park was converted into a terrace and the local printer was selling programmes.

EVEN STEVENS
Official programme
Price 50p
Even Stevens v Blackpool FC
(featuring Wayne 'Zigzag' Travis)
FA CUP FIRST ROUND

Every child and teacher from Wayne's school was there—even the head. The whole nation tuned in to hear the report at the end of Grandstand.

'Two seconds into the game and the non-leaguers were 1–nil down. It appeared to be a walk-over for the one-time cup-winning club of the great Sir Stanley Matthews. But how that mighty name suffered today, as Blackpool experienced four early send-offs for unclean tackling!

'With Blackpool down to seven men, Even Stevens were in with a chance. But Blackpool had further surprises in store, when four forwards formed a rugby scrum and charged towards the goal with the ball tucked under one of the jerseys. Early bath for them too, and Blackpool were down to three men.

'Even Stevens equalized after half-time. And then, in what must be one of the upsets of the century, young Wayne Travis took control of the ball.

'Kicked from well outside Blackpool's penalty area, the ball made an astonishing triple-bouncing journey up the pitch. I couldn't really see from where I was, but somehow or other it landed up in the Blackpool net.

'At the final whistle it was 2–1 to Even Stevens. They're into round two, and they'll be celebrating down in Hackney tonight, I can tell you.'

That night was the greatest night of Wayne's life and he ate two kebabs, fourteen jaffa cakes, four Jamaican patties, eight slices of celebration cake, fourteen packets of crisps, and twelve chocolate bars at the celebration party in Shakespeare Street.

The next draw turned out to be against non-league Waterloo Station Rovers—what a let-down! It would have been much more fun to be beaten by one of the league teams.

Wayne went back to playing 23-a-side football in the alley behind school. He didn't practise his Hedley Carlton Triple-Bounce Goal.

A few weeks later, while Wayne was doing his homework and Dad was dozing in his armchair . . .

'. . . Semi-professional football club, Waterloo Station Rovers, has been forced to close down . . . in a statement . . . fraud . . . fifty thousand pounds missing . . . in court tomorrow . . . punched the manager . . . police . . . no further part in the FA Cup.'

Wayne's dad woke up and leapt to his feet so suddenly that he put his back out.

'That means we're through the second round of the FA Cup! If only I could get myself fit in time.'

At first Wayne thought—brilliant! Playing one of the big boys. But then he thought, What if Dad *does* get fit in time?

Wouldn't that mean he'd lose his place in the team? And hadn't Nigel Fiddle rung from Poland (or Bulgaria) the other day to say he was on his way back with a lorry load of new shoes and boots?

When Even Stevens were drawn away against Manchester United in the third round, even Moira Stewart was stunned to silence.

Manchester United?

Old Trafford?

A crowd of over forty thousand?

Live coverage on TV?

Maybe they should simply bow out now before nerves and humiliation got the better of them. Instead, what happened was one of the most curious and extraordinary games of football in the world.

Erkan Hussein may not have been the world's greatest captain, but he knew a thing or two about football. In the weeks leading up to the game he racked his brains and, by the day of the Big Match, he had a plan.

In the dressing room at Old Trafford he revealed it for the first time. (He drew it in the steam on the dressing room window.)

As the teams ran out on to the pitch, the roar that hit

them nearly knocked Wayne over. He was on the subs bench today, next to his dad who had a bad toe. (Nigel, who was back from Romania, had said, 'Either I play or you lot don't get the new boots.')

Then came the Erkan Hussein plan.

'. . . an amazing sight here at Old Trafford. The non-leaguers are in a semi-circle guarding their own goal. The United forwards are trying to fight their way through but there really is no way round this.

'Man. United's captain has called a conference . . .

'. . . And Even Stevens have broken out of the semi-circle. They're taking the ball upfield . . . and they've scored! And Man. United haven't even noticed. What an amazing move!'

And 1–nil was where the score stayed until the final whistle. One of the smallest clubs in the world had beaten one of the biggest.

That night the World Football Council had an emergency meeting in the Eiffel Tower and changed the rules of football so that it could never happen again:

Rule Number 457
Semi circles and defences.
Teams are not allowed to form a defensive ring round the goal.

Even Stevens were through to Round 4, away to Bristol Rovers. It was never going to be an easy game after the scandal at Old Trafford. The *SCUM* paper wrote,

---

Even Cheaters
CHEATS!!!
Dirty, cheating crooks, Even Stevens, go to Bristol today and let's hope they get well and truly crushed.
BEAT THE CHEATS!!

'Look at this, Dad,' cried Wayne.

'Football's a cruel game, son,' said Dad.

But Wayne was back in the team. (Nigel Fiddle had to go back to Romania—or was it Estonia? He had forgotten to pick up the bootlaces.)

Two minutes into the game, Bristol's Jimmy Rack left the field.

'Bristol Rovers will not be fielding any substitutes today: David Dover's wife, Eileen, has gone into hospital to have a baby and David's with her. Best of luck, Eileen! And—amazing coincidence—Doug Bitnearer's wife is having a baby too—best of luck, Lena!'

Three minutes later, three more went . . .

'Well, here's a turn up for the books. Jimmy Rack's missus, Anna, has just been taken to hospital. They're expecting their third child. Best of luck, Anna!'

One minute later . . .

'Dennis Pond's wife, Lily, George Showers's wife, April, and Pete Bee's wife, May, have all just been taken to hospital to have their babies.

'Well, there's certainly going to be a few more little Rovers in town tonight. Good luck Laura Norder, Ruby Redd and the rest . . .!'

Bristol Rovers were down to one man. Even Stevens won 45–nil.

Even Stevens were through to the fifth round of the FA Cup, with only sixteen clubs left in. Life was supposed to go on as usual for the players, but it wasn't easy.

Erkan's leather factory started making leather badges:

DON'T BE ODD!

GO WITH THE EVENS!

Satoshi regularly appeared on satellite TV to Japan.

Linton was Number 1 in the Rap Charts with 'Believin' Even Stevens'.

And Wayne . . . ? Well, the whole school was doing a project on football.

Even Stevens featured in the papers almost every day.

SCUMsport

FA CUP FIFTH ROUND

Win the pools with Harry Bigforest

WIMBLEDON V. EVEN STEVENS

This should be a pushover for Wimbledon. Their superior long ball game should easily penetrate the non-leaguer's defence, though Stevens's captain, 'Tesco' Hussein, tells me he's got something special up his sleeve (and it's not just his arm).

And indeed he had. When Even Stevens ran out on to the pitch for the game, everything looked normal. But the moment the whistle blew, Even Stevens turned their backs on the Wimbledon goal and played the whole game running backwards.

Wimbledon's Greg Walnut tackled Moira.

The ref blew him up for tackling from behind.

Ron Cobnut tackled Donna.

The ref blew him up for tackling from behind.

It was unbeatable. Wimbledon were completely outplayed.

FINAL SCORE
Wimbledon 0, Even Stevens 3

That night the World Football Council had an emergency meeting at Niagara Falls:

Rule Number 458
Running backwards.
No team shall spend more than two minutes running, shooting, passing, or playing set-pieces backwards.

Even Stevens were through to the last eight.

Moira was a guest on breakfast television, and Linton appeared in a quiz show. Every single member of the team was involved in something, from opening supermarkets to charity work.

Wayne was finding it hard to concentrate in school. Some of his mates were really jealous.

'I'm better at football than you, Wayne. I ought to be playing for the Stevens.'

'Maybe you are, but you don't live at an even number in Shakespeare Street, do you? So, hard cheese!'

In the sixth round Even Stevens were drawn at home to Aston Villa.

Now, you probably would agree that Even Stevens had had a bit of luck so far in the tournament. But what happened next was unheard of in the history of football.

Aston Villa got lost. That's right, lost.

As Wayne told his dad, 'That's hard luck on the Villa fans, Dad.'

'Football's a cruel game, son,' said Dad.

They just couldn't find their way to the Mammoth Hypermarket Astroturf. Perhaps the trouble was that Mammoth were doing rather good business and had opened up twelve new stores between Aston Villa and Hackney, but whatever it was, Villa never made it to the match.

That night, the draw was made on TV.

'We're through to the semi-finals! Liverpool versus Even Stevens!'

Wayne was over the moon.

That week, Even Stevens trained hard. Erkan had run out of ideas and the intrepid team were just glad that they had lasted long enough to meet such brilliant opponents.

That week, Liverpool played hard. On Monday they played Bayern Munich in the fourth round of the European Cup. It was a draw, replay Thursday night.

On Tuesday they played in the fifth round of the Humbellow Cup. It was a draw, replay Friday night.

On Thursday they played in the replay of the fourth round of the European Cup. It went to extra time. They lost.

On Friday they played in the replay of the fifth round of the Humbellow Cup. It went to extra time. They lost.

Anyone could have beaten Liverpool that day.

Final score: Liverpool 0, Even Stevens 6.

'Isn't that . . .' began Wayne.

'Football's a cruel game, son,' said Dad.

Yes, the amazing news was that Even Stevens, the team from Shakespeare Street, Hackney, were in the FA Cup Final.

The bad news was that Nigel Fiddle was back from Lithuania with another lot of boots, and he wanted to play. Wayne's dad's back was finally on the mend, too. Things didn't look good for Wayne.

At last the great day arrived.

THE FINAL

4 mins

'. . . Spurs launch an attack down the middle. Sparrow sprays it out on the right flank to Doddle. A beautiful cross; it's beaten Rodney Travis! Greyleg has run through to nod it in. 1–nil to Tottenham, but there was a suspicion of off-side. Let's look at it again on the replay . . . and yes, definitely offside . . . Bobby?'

'Absolutely.'

22 mins

'. . . Doddle jinxing his way round the Stevens' defence. Postlethwaite's got it back, and, oh, that's a foul, surely? Referee waves play on. Doddle takes it on the left foot. Top corner. It's a goal!! 2–nil to

28

Tottenham. Let's look at that again on the replay . . . and yes, that's a foul, surely . . . Bobby?'
   'Absolutely.'

43 mins
'Greyleg takes the corner, and it's Doddle with the diving header. Fantastic save by Bradley. No! The referee's given a goal!! Let's look at that again. Oh no, you can see Bradley held it. Oh dear me, the third controversial goal, Bobby . . .'
   'Absolutely.'

Second half
51 mins
'. . . And Travis is down!'

56 mins
'. . . and Wayne Travis is on. Eyebulge towers over him, but Travis gets it away. Extraordinary— it's turning towards the penalty area. It's heading for goal. Spreadeagle's got it covered . . . Oh, no he hasn't. It's in! It's a goal! That's 3–1 to Spurs. The pitch must be a little uneven today, Bobby?'
   'Absolutely.'

79 mins
'. . . Donna Louis fairly steaming through mid-field there. Travis takes it. Oh, it's a tame one. Bounces early, takes a strange turn. Slug's covering—he's misjudged it. Greyleg will clear off the line, surely . . . No—it's in. It's a goal!! Sensational! 3–2.
   'The referee ought to look at the stitching on the ball, don't you agree, Bobby?'
   'Absolutely.'

The seconds were ticking away. The ref was looking at his watch. If only Wayne could get the ball once more.
   'Give it to Zigzag!' came a shout.

As the ref put the whistle in his mouth, Satoshi slipped Wayne the ball.

Wayne took a huge swipe at it. Off it went. One bounce, two bounces, three bounces.

It was going to be a goal . . .

It was going to be the equalizer . . .

. . . Then the whistle went.

Half a second later the ball was in the net. Goal but no goal.

No extra time.

End of game.

Spurs had won the cup.

Then an odd thing happened. Instead of letting the losing team collect their medals, the Spurs captain ran up to collect the FA Cup. He brought it back down to the pitch and gave Erkan the lid.

'You were robbed, mate,' he said.

Everyone agreed it was the most extraordinary FA Cup Final in football history. People all over the world argued about the final score.

Wayne finally got his wish and appeared on the new *Goals of the Century* video.

And today people still study Wayne's kicks to see exactly what happened. The argument rages.

But Wayne Travis and the Even Stevens FC squad will never forget that day.

'You'd have beaten them with that Hedley Carlton Triple-Bounce, son, if you'd had the chance,' sighed Dad.

'Well . . .' said Wayne, 'football's a cruel game, Dad!'

Football!

Football! *Football!*
The boys want the entire playground
and we're left squashed
against the broken fence.
Why don't the teachers stop them?
  Why?
Haven't they got *any* sense?

My friend Anna
ran across the tarmac. Smack!
Got the football right on her nose.
Blood all over her face.
Why don't the teachers do something?
  Why?
It's a disgrace, *a disgrace!*

Those boys . . . I mean
they're like hooligans.
CHEL-SEA! CHEL-SEA! they chant
morning, noon and night.
The teacher on duty does . . . nothing.
  Why?
It's just, it's just not right.

We complain bitterly
but the duty teacher says,
'Go see the Head. He's in charge.'
Him! He's *useless.* YOU-ESS-LESS!
When we ask him to ban football
  Why,
oh why, can't he just say 'Yes'?

Wes Magee

31

Denis Law

I live at 14 Stanhope Street,
Me mum, me dad and me,
And three of us have made a gang,
John Stokes and Trev and me.

Our favourite day is Saturday;
We go Old Trafford way
And wear red colours in our coats
To watch United play.

We always stand behind the goal
In the middle of the roar.
The others come to see the game—
I come for Denis Law.

His red sleeves flap around his wrists,
He's built all thin and raw,
But the toughest backs don't stand a chance
When the ball's near Denis Law.

He's a whiplash when he's in control,
He can swivel like an eel,
And twist and sprint in such a way
It makes defences reel.

And when he's hurtling for the goal
I know he's got to score.
Defences may stop normal men—
They can't stop Denis Law.

We all race home when full time blows
To kick a tennis ball,
And Trafford Park is our back-yard,
And the stand is next door's wall.

Old Stokesey shouts, 'I'm Jimmy Greaves,'
And scores against the door,
And Trev shouts: 'I'll be Charlton,'—
But I am Denis Law.

Gareth Owen

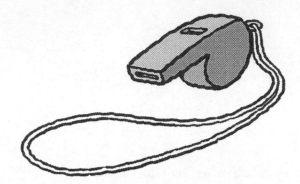

The Football Match

BARRY HINES

He walked into the changing room as clean and shining as a boy down for breakfast on his seaside holidays. The other boys were packed into the aisles between the rows of pegs, their hanging clothes partitioning the room into corridors. Mr Sugden was passing slowly across one end of the room, looking down the corridors and counting the boys as they changed. He was wearing a violet tracksuit. The top was embellished with cloth badges depicting numerous crests and qualifications, and on the breast a white athlete carried the Olympic torch. The legs were tucked into new white football socks, neatly folded at his ankles, and his football boots were polished as black and shiny as the bombs used by assassins in comic strips. The laces binding them had been scrubbed white, and both boots had been fastened identically: two loops of the foot and one of the ankle, and tied in a neat bow under the tab at the back.

He finished counting and rolled a football off the window sill into his hand. The leather was rich with dubbin, and the new orange lace nipped the slit as firmly as a row of surgical stitches. He tossed it up and caught it on the ends of his fingers, then turned round to Billy.

'Skyving again, Casper?'

'No, sir, Mr Farthing wanted me; he's been talking to me.'

'I bet that was stimulating for him, wasn't it?'

'What does that mean, sir?'

'The conversation, lad, what do you think it means?'

'No, sir, that word, stimult . . . stimult-ting.'

'Stimulating you fool, S-T-I-M-U-L-A-T-I-N-G, stimulating!'

'Yes, sir.'

'Well, get changed, lad, you're two weeks late already!'

He lifted the elastic webbing of one cuff and rotated his fist to look at his watch on the underside of his wrist.

'Some of us want a game even if you don't.'

'I've no kit, sir.'

Mr Sugden stepped back and slowly looked Billy up and down, his top lip curling.

'Casper, you make me *sick*.'

'*Sick*' penetrated the hubbub, which immediately decreased as the boys stopped their own conversations and turned their attention to Mr Sugden and Billy.

'Every lesson it's the same old story, "Please, sir, I've no kit."'

The boys tittered at his whipped-dog whining impersonation.

'Every lesson for four years! And in all that time you've made no attempt whatsoever to get any kit, you've skyved and scrounged and borrowed and . . .'

He tried this lot on one breath, and his ruddy complexion heightened and glowed like a red balloon as he held his breath and fought for another verb.

'. . . and . . . *beg* . . .' The balloon burst and the pronunciation of the verb disintegrated. 'Why is it that everyone else can get some but you can't?'

'I don't know, sir. My mother won't buy me any. She says it's a waste of money, especially now that I'm leaving.'

'You haven't been leaving for four years, have you?'
'No, sir.'
'You could have bought some out of your spending money, couldn't you?'
'I don't like football, sir.'
'What's that got to do with it?'
'I don't know, sir. Anyway I don't get enough.'
'Get a job then. I don't—'
'I've got one, sir.'
'Well then! You get paid, don't you?'
'Yes, sir. But I have to gi' it to my mam. I'm still payin' her for my fines, like instalments every week.'

Mr Sugden bounced the ball on Billy's head, compressing his neck into his shoulders.

'Well, you should keep out of trouble then, lad, and then—'
'I haven't been in trouble, sir, not—'
'Shut up, lad! Shut up, before you drive me crackers!'

He hit Billy twice with the ball, holding it between both hands as though he was murdering him with a boulder. The rest of the class grinned behind each other's backs, or placed their fingers over their mouths to suppress the laughter gathering there. They watched Mr Sugden rush into his changing room, and began to giggle, stopping immediately he reappeared waving a pair of giant blue drawers.

'Here, Casper, get them on!'

He wanged them across the room, and Billy caught them flying over his head, then held them up for inspection as though he was contemplating buying. The class roared. They would have made Billy two suits and an overcoat.

'They'll not fit me, sir.'

The class roared again and even Billy had to smile. There was only Mr Sugden not amused.

'What are you talking about, lad? You can get them on, can't you?'

'Yes, sir.'

'Well, they fit you then! Now get changed, *quick*.'

Billy found an empty peg and hung his jacket on it. He was immediately enclosed in a tight square as two lines of boys formed up, one on each side of him between the parallel curtains of clothing. He sat down on the long bench covering the shoe racks, and worked his jeans over his pumps. Mr Sugden broke one side of the square and stood over him.

'And you want your underpants and vest off.'

'I don't wear 'em, sir.'

As he reached up to hang his trousers on the peg, his shirt tail lifted, revealing his bare cheeks, which looked as smooth and bony as two white billiard balls. He stepped into the shorts and pulled them up to his waist. The legs reached halfway down his shins. He pulled the waist up to his neck and his knees just slid into view. Boys pointed at them, shouting and laughing into each other's faces, and other boys who were still changing rushed to the scene, jumping up on the benches or parting the curtains to see through. And at the centre of it all, Billy, like a brave little clown, was busy trying to make them fit, and Sugden was looking at him as though it was his fault for being too small for them.

'Roll them down and don't be so foolish. You're too daft to laugh at, Casper.'

No one else thought so. Billy started to roll them down from his chest, each tuck shortening the legs and gathering the material round his waist in a floppy blue tyre.

'That'll do. Let's have you all out now.'

He opened the door and led them down the corridor and out into the yard. Some boys waited until he had gone, then they took a run and had a good slide up to the door, rotating slowly as they slid, and finishing up facing the way they had come. Those with rubber studs left long black streaks on the tiles. The plastic and nailed leather studs cut through the veneer and scored deep scratches in the vinyl. When they reached the yard, the pad of the rubber studs on the concrete hardly differed from that in the changing room or the corridor, but the clatter produced by the nailed and plastic studs had a hollow, more metallic ring.

The cold caught Billy's breath as he stepped outside. He stopped dead, glanced round as though looking to escape, then set off full belt, shouting, across the concrete on to the field. Mr Sugden set off after him.

'Casper! Shut up, lad! What are you trying to do, disrupt the whole school?'

He gained on Billy, and as he drew near swiped at him with his flat hand. Billy, watching the blows, zigzagged out of reach, just ahead of them.

'I'm frozen, sir! I'm shoutin' to keep warm!'

'Well, don't shout at me then! I'm not a mile away!'

They were shouting at each other as though they were aboard ship in a gale. Mr Sugden tried to swat him again. Billy side-stepped, and threw him off balance. So he slowed to a walk and turned round, blowing his whistle and beckoning the others to hurry up.

'Come on, you lot! Hurry up!'

They started to run at speeds ranging from jogging to sprinting, and arrived within a few seconds of each other on the senior football pitch.

'Line up on the halfway line and let's get two sides picked!'

They lined up, jumping and running on the spot, those with long sleeves clutching the cuffs in their hands, those without massaging their goosey arms.

'Tibbut, come out here and be the other captain.'

Tibbut walked out and stood facing the line, away from Mr Sugden.

'I'll have first pick, Tibbut.'

'That's not right, sir.'

'Why isn't it?'

' 'Cos you'll get all the best players.'

'Rubbish, lad.'

' 'Course you will, sir. It's not fair.'

'Tibbut. Do you want to play football? Or do you want to get dressed and go and do some maths?'

'Play football, sir.'

'Right then, stop moaning and start picking. I'll have Anderson.'

He turned away from Tibbut and pointed to a boy who was standing on one of the intersections of the centre circle and the halfway line. Anderson walked off this cross and stood behind him. Tibbut scanned the line, considering his choice.

'I'll have Purdey.'

'Come on then, Ellis.'

Each selection altered the structure of the line. When Tibbut had been removed from the centre, all the boys sidestepped to fill the gap. The same happened when Anderson went from near one end. But when Purdey and Ellis, who had been standing side by side, were removed, the boys at their shoulders stood still, therefore dividing the original line into two. These new lines were swiftly segmented as more boys were chosen, leaving no trace of the first major division, just half a dozen boys looking across spaces at each other; reading from left to right: a fat boy; an arm's length away, two friends, one tall with glasses, the other short with a hare-lip; then a space of two yards and Billy; a boy space away from him, a thin boy with a crew-cut and a spotty face; and right away from these, at the far end of the line, another fat boy. Spotty Crew-Cut was halfway between the two fat boys, therefore half of the length of the line was occupied by five of the boys. The far fat boy was the next to go, which halved the length of the line and left Spotty Crew-Cut as one of the end markers.

Tibbut then selected the tall friend with glasses. Mr Sugden immediately selected his partner. They separated gradually as they walked away from the line, parting finally to enter their respective teams. And then there were three: Fatty, Billy, and Spotty Crew-Cut, blushing across at each other while the captains considered. Tibbut picked Crew-Cut. He dashed forward into the anonymity of his team. Fatty stood grinning. Billy stared down at the earth. After long deliberation Mr Sugden chose Billy, leaving Tibbut with Hobson's choice; but before either Billy or Fatty could move towards their teams, Mr Sugden was already turning away and shouting instructions.

'Right! We'll play down hill!'

The team broke for their appropriate halves, and while they were arguing their claims for positions, Mr Sugden jogged to the sideline, dropped the ball, and took off his tracksuit. Underneath he was wearing a crisp red football shirt with white cuffs and a white band round the neck. A big white 9 filled most of the back, whiter than his white nylon shorts, which showed a slight fleshy tint through the material. He pulled his socks up, straightened the ribs, then took a fresh roll of half inch bandage from his tracksuit and ripped off two lengths. The torn bandage packet, the cup of its structure still intact, blew away over the turf like the damaged shell of a dark blue egg. Mr Sugden used the lengths of bandage to secure his stockings just below the knees, then he folded his tracksuit neatly on the ground, looked down at himself, and walked on to the pitch carrying the ball like a plum pudding on the tray of his hand. Tibbut, standing on the centre circle, with his hands down his shorts, winked at his Left Winger and waited for Mr Sugden to approach.

'Who are you today, sir, Liverpool?'

'Rubbish, lad! Don't you know your club colours yet?'

'Liverpool are red, aren't they, sir?'

'Yes, but they're all red, shirts, shorts, and stockings. These are Manchester United's colours.'

' 'Course they are, sir, I forgot. What position are you playing?'

Mr Sugden turned his back on him to show him the number 9.

'Bobby Charlton. I thought you were usually Denis Law when you were Manchester United.'

'It's too cold to play as a striker today. I'm scheming this morning, all over the field like Charlton.'

'Law plays all over, sir. He's not only a striker.'

'He doesn't link like Charlton.'

'Better player though, sir.'

Sugden shook his head. 'No, he's been badly off form recently.'

'Makes no odds, he's still a better player. He can settle a game in two minutes.'

'Are you trying to tell *me* about football, Tibbut?'

'No, sir.'

'Well, shut up then. Anyway Law's in the wash this week.'

He placed the ball on the centre spot and looked round at his team. There was only Billy out of position. He was standing between the full backs, the three of them forming a domino : : : pattern with the half backs. The goal was empty. Mr Sugden pointed at it.

'There's no one in goal!'

His team looked round to confirm this observation, but Tibbut's team had beaten them to it by just looking straight ahead.

'Casper! What position are you supposed to be playing?'

Billy looked to the Right Back, the Left Back, the Right Back again. Neither of them supplied the answer, so he answered the question himself.

'I don't know, sir. Inside Right?'

This answer made 1: Mr Sugden angry; 2: the boys laugh.

'Don't talk ridiculous, lad! How can you be playing Inside Right back there?'

He looked up at the sky.

'God help us; fifteen years old and still doesn't know the positions of a football team!'

He levelled one arm at Billy.

'Get in goal, lad!'

'Oh, sir! I can't goal. I'm no good.'

'Now's your chance to learn then, isn't it?'

'I'm fed up o' goin' in goal. I go in every week.'

Billy turned round and looked at the goal as though it was the portal leading into the gladiatorial arena.

'Don't stand looking, lad. Get in there!'

'Well, don't blame me then, when I let 'em all through.'

'Of course I'll blame you, lad! Who do you expect me to blame?'

Billy cursed him quietly all the way back to the nets.

Sugden (commentator): 'And both teams are lined up for the kick off in this vital fifth-round cup-tie, Manchester United versus . . .?' Sugden (teacher): 'Who are we playing, Tibbut?'

'Er . . . we'll be Liverpool, sir.'

'You can't be Liverpool.'

'Why not, sir?'

'I've told you once, they're too close to Manchester United's colours aren't they?'

Tibbut massaged his brow with his fingertips, and under this guise of thinking, glanced round at his team: Goalkeeper, green polo. Right Back, blue and white stripes. Left Back, green and white quarters. Right Half, white cricket. Centre Half, all blue. Left Half, all yellow. Right Wing, orange and green rugby. Inside Right, black T. Centre Forward, blue denim tab collar. Tibbut, red body white sleeves. Left Wing, all blue.

'We'll be Spurs then, sir. There'll be no clash of colours then.'

'. . . And it's Manchester United v. Spurs in this vital fifth-round cup-tie.'

Mr Sugden (referee) sucked his whistle and stared at his watch, waiting for the second finger to twitch back up to twelve. 5 4 3 2. He dropped his wrist and blew. Anderson received the ball from him, sidestepped a tackle from Tibbut then cut it diagonally between two opponents into a space to his left. Sugden (player) running into this space, raised his left foot to trap it, but the ball rolled under his studs. He veered left, caught it, and started to cudgel it upfield in a travesty of a dribble, sending it too far ahead each time he touched it, so that by the time he had progressed twenty yards, he had crash-tackled it back from three Spurs defenders. His left winger, unmarked and lonely out on the touchline, called for the ball, Sugden heard him, looked at him, then kicked the ball hard along the ground towards him. But even though the wingman started to spring as soon as he read its line, it still shot out of play a good ten yards in front of him. He slithered to a stop and whipped round.

'Hey up, sir! What do you think I am?'

'You should have been moving, lad. You'd have caught it then.'

'What do you think I wa' doing, standing still?'

'It was a perfectly good ball!'

'Ar, for a whippet perhaps!'

'Don't argue with me, lad! And get that ball fetched!'

The ball had rolled and stopped on the roped-off cricket square. The left winger left the pitch and walked towards it. He scissor-jumped the rope, picked the ball up off the lush lawn, then volleyed it straight back on to the pitch without bouncing it once on the intervening stretch of field.

Back in the goal, Billy was giant-striding along the goal line, counting the number of strides from post to post: five and a bit. He turned, propelled himself off the post and jump-strode across to the other side: five. After three more attempts he reduced this record to four and a half, then he returned along the line, heel-toe, heel-toeing it: thirty pump lengths.

After fourteen minutes' play he touched the ball for the first time. Tibbut, dribbling in fast, pushed the ball between Mr Sugden's legs, ran round him and delivered the ball out to his right winger, who took it in his stride, beat his Full Back and centred for Tibbut, who had continued his run, to outjump Mr Sugden and head the ball firmly into the top right-hand corner of the goal. Billy watched it fly in, way up on his left, then he turned round and picked it up from under the netting.

'Come on, Casper! Make an effort, lad!'

'I couldn't save that, sir.'

'You could have tried.'

'What for, sir, when I knew I couldn't save it?'

'We're playing this game to win you know, lad.'

'I know, sir.'

'Well, try then!'

He held his hands out to receive the ball. Billy obliged, but as it left his hand the wet leather skidded off his skin and it dropped short in the mud, between them. He ran out to retrieve it, but Sugden had already started towards it, and when Billy saw the stare of his eyes and the set of his jaw as he ran at the ball, he stopped and dropped down, and the ball missed him and went over him, back into the net. He knelt up, his left arm, left side and left leg striped with mud.

'What wa' that for, sir?'

'Slack work, lad. Slack work.'

He retrieved the ball himself, and carried it quickly back to the centre for the restart. Billy stood up, a mud pack stuck to each knee. He pulled his shirt sleeve round and started to furrow the mud with his finger nails.

'Look at this lot. I've to keep this shirt on an' all after.'

The Right Back was drawn by this lament, but was immediately distracted by a chorus of warning shouts, and when he turned round he saw the ball running loose in his direction. He ran at it head down, and toed it far up field, showing no interest in its flight or destination, but turning to commiserate with Billy almost as soon as it had left his boot. It soared over the halfway line, and Sugden started to chase. It bounced, once, twice, then rolled out towards the touchline. He must catch it and the rest of his forward line moved up in anticipation of the centre. But the ball, decelerating rapidly as though it wanted to be caught, still crossed the line before he could reach it. His disappointed Forwards muttered amongst themselves as they trooped back out of the penalty area.

'He should have caught that, easy.'

'He's like a chuffing carthorse.'

'Look at him, he's knackered.'

'Hopeless tha means.'

Tibbut picked the ball up for the throw in.

'Hard luck, sir.'

Sugden, hands on hips, chest heaving, had his Right Back in focus a good thirty seconds before he had sufficient control over his respiration to remonstrate with him.

'Come on, lad! Find a man with this ball! Don't just kick it anywhere!'

The Right Back, his back turned, continued his conversation with Billy.

'*Sparrow!*'

'What, sir?'

'I'm talking to you, lad!'

'Yes, sir.'

'Well, pay attention then and get a grip of your game. We're losing, lad.'

'Yes, sir.'

Manchester United equalized soon after when the referee awarded them a penalty. Sugden scored.

At the other end of the pitch, Billy was busy with the netting. He was standing with his back to the play,

clawing the fibres and growling like a little lion. He
stuck a paw through a square and pawed at a visitor,
withdrew it and stalked across his cage. The only other
exhibit was the herd of multi-coloured cross-breeds
gambolling around the ball behind him. The rest of the
grounds were deserted. The main body of the collection
was housed in the building across the fields, and all
round the fields a high wire fence had been constructed.
Round the top of the fence strands of barbed wire were
affixed to inward-leaning angle-irons. Round the
bottom, a ridge of shaggy grass grew where the mower
had missed, and underneath the wire the grass had been
cut in a severe fringe by the concrete flags of the
pavement. The road curved round the field in a
crescent, and across the road the row of council houses
mirrored this exact curve. Field Crescent.

Billy gripped a post between both hands, inserted
one raised foot into a square in the side netting, then,
using this as a stirrup, heaved himself up and grabbed
hold of the cross-bar. He hand-over-handed it to the
middle and rested, swinging loosely backwards and
forwards with his legs together. Then he let go with
one hand and started to scratch his arm pits, kicking
his legs and imitating chimp sounds. The bar shook,
and the rattling of the bolts turned several heads, and
soon all the boys were watching him, the game
forgotten.

'Casper! Casper, get down, lad! What do you think
you are, an ape?'

'No, sir. I'm just keeping warm.'

'Well, get down then, before I come and make you
red hot!'

Billy grasped the bar again with both hands,
adjusted his grip, and began to swing: forward and
back, forward and back, increasing momentum with
thrusts of his legs. Forward and back, upwards and
back, legs horizontal as he swung upwards and back.
Horizontal and back, horizontal both ways, hands

leaving bar at the top of each swing. Forward and back, just one more time; then a rainbow flight down, and a landing knees bent.

He needed no steps or staggering to correct his balance, but stood up straight, smiling; the cross-bar still quivering.

Applause broke out. Sugden silenced it.

'Right, come on then, let's get on with this game.'

The score: still 1–1.

1–2. When Billy, shielding his face, deflected a stinger up on to the cross-bar, and it bounced down behind him and over the line.

2–2. When the referee, despite protests, allowed a goal by Anderson to count, even though he appeared to score it from an offside position.

A dog appeared at the edge of the field, a lean black mongrel, as big as an Alsatian, sniffing around the bottom of the fence on the pavement side. A second later it was inside, bounding across the field to join the game. It skidded round the ball, barking. The boy on the ball got off it, quick. The dog lay on its front legs, back curved, tail up continuing the line of its body. The boys ganged up at a distance, 'yarring' and threatening, but every time one of them moved towards it, the dog ran at him, jumping and barking, scattering the lot of them before turning and running back to the ball.

The boys were as excited as children playing 'Mr Wolf'. Carefully they closed in, then, when one of them made his effort to retrieve the ball, and the dog retaliated, they all scattered, screaming, to form up again twenty yards away and begin a new advance. If Mr Sugden had had a gun, Mr Wolf would have been dead in no time.

'Whose is it? Who does it belong to?' (From the back of the mob as it advanced, leading it when they retreated.) 'Somebody go and fetch some cricket bats from the storeroom, they'll shift it.'

In the excitement nobody took any notice of him, so he looked round and saw Billy, who was stamping patterns in the goalmouth mud.

'Casper!'

'What, sir?'

'Come here!'

'What, sir?'

'Go and fetch half a dozen cricket bats from the games store.'

'Cricket bats, sir! What, in this weather?'

'No, you fool! To shift that dog—it's ruining the game.'

'You don't need cricket bats to do that, sir.'

'What do you need then, dynamite?'

'It'll not hurt you.'

'I'm not giving it a chance. I'd sooner take meat away from a starving lion than take the ball away from that thing.'

The dog was playing with the ball, holding it between its front paws, and with its head on one side, trying to bite it. However its jaws were too narrow, and each time it closed them its teeth pushed the ball forward out of reach. Then it shuffled after it, growling and rumbling in its throat. Billy walked forward, patting one thigh and clicking his tongue on the roof of his mouth. The other boys got down to their marks.

'Come on then, lad. Come on.'

It came. Bouncing up to his chest and down and round him. He reached out and scuffled its head each time it bounced up to his hand.

'What's up wi'thi? What's up then, you big daft sod?'

It rested its front paws on his chest and barked bright-eyed into his face, its tongue turning up at the edges and slithering in and out as it breathed. Billy fondled its ears, then walked away from it, making it drop down on all fours.

'Come on then, lad. Come on. Where do you want me to take him, sir?'

'Anywhere, lad. Anywhere as long as you get it off this field.'

'Do you want me to find out where it lives, sir, and take it home? I can be dressed in two ticks.'

'No. No, just get it off the field and get back in your goal.'

Billy hooked his finger under the dog's collar and led it firmly towards the school, talking quietly to it all the time.

When he returned they were leading 3–2.

A few minutes later they were level 3–3.

'What's the matter, Casper, are you scared of the ball?'

Mr Sugden studied his watch, as the ball was returned to him at the centre spot.

'Right then, the next goal's the winner!'

One to make and the match to win.

End to end play. Excitement. Thrills. OOOO! Arrr! Goal! No! It was over the line, sir! Play on!

Billy snatched the ball up, ran forward, and volleyed it up the field. He turned round and hopped back, pulling a sucked lemon face.

'Bloody hell, it's like lead, that ball. It's just like gettin' t'stick across your feet.'

He stood stork fashion and manipulated his foot. Every time he turned his toes up water squeezed into the folds of the instep of his pump.

'Bugger me. I'm not kicking that again.'

He placed the foot lightly to the ground and tested his weight on it.

'I feel champion, bones broke in one foot, frostbite in t'other.'

He unrolled his shorts up to his neck and pushed his arms down inside them.

'Come on, Sugden, blow that bloody whistle, I'm frozen.'

The game continued. Sugden shot over the bar. Seconds later he prevented Tibbut from shooting by tugging his shirt. Penalty! Play on.

Billy sighted the school behind one outstretched thumb and obliterated it by drawing the thumb slowly to his eye. A young midget walked from behind the nail. Billy opened his other eye and dropped his hand. More midgets were leaving the midget building, walking down the midget drive to the midget gates. Billy ran out to the edge of the penalty area, his arms back at attention down his shorts.

'Bell's gone, sir! They're comin' out!'

'Never mind the bell, get back in your goal!'

'I'm on first sitting, sir. I'll miss my dinner.'

'I thought I told you to swap sittings when you had games.'

'I forgot, sir.'

'Well you'd better forget about your dinner then.'

He turned back to the game, then did a double take.

'And get your arms out of your shorts, lad! You look as if you've had Thalidomide!'

Play developed at the other end. Billy stayed on the edge of the penalty area, forming a trio with his Full Backs.

'How can I stop to second dinners when I've to go home an' feed my hawk?'

All the toys had disappeared from the playground, some of them growing into boys as they walked up Field Crescent and passed level with the pitch. They shouted encouragement through the wire, then shrank and disappeared round the curve.

They were replaced by a man and a woman approaching in the same direction, on opposite pavements. The man was wearing a grey suit, the woman a green coat, and as they drew level with the field they merged on to the same plane, and were suddenly pursued by a red car. Three blocks of colour, red, grey, and green, travelling on the same plane, in the same direction, and at different speeds. Stop. Red, grey, and green. Above the green of the field, against the red of the houses, and below the grey of the sky. Start. The car wove between the two pedestrians, drawing its noise between them like a steel hawser. A few seconds later the man passed the woman, grey-green merging momentarily, and seconds later the woman opened a garden gate and disappeared from the scene, leaving the man isolated on the Crescent. Silence. Then the burst of a motor bike, Rrm! Rrm! Revving behind the houses, fading, to allow a thunk of the ball. A call, an echo, an empty yard. A sheet of paper captured against the wire by the wind.

12.15 p.m. The winning goal suddenly became important, no more laughter, no more joking, everybody working. For most of the game most of the boys had been as fixed as buttons on a pinball machine, sparking into life only when the nucleus of footballers amongst them had occasionally shuttled the ball into their defined areas: mere props to the play. Now they were all playing. Both teams playing as units, and positions were taken seriously. In possession they moved and called for the ball from spaces. Out of possession they marked and tackled hard to win it back. A move provoked a counter move, which in turn determined moves made by players in other segments of the pitch. The ball was a magnet, exerting the strongest pull on the players nearest to it, and still strong enough to activate the players farthest away.

12.20 p.m. Billy jump, jump, jumped on the line. 'Score, for Christ's sake somebody score.' Tick tick tick tick. Sugden missed again. He's blind, he's bleedin' blind. Sugden was crimson and sweating like a drayhorse, and boys began to accelerate smoothly past him, well wide of him, well clear of his scything legs and shirt-grabbing fists.

Manchester United came under serious pressure. Sugden retreated to his own penalty area, tackling and clearing and hoping for a breakaway. But back it came, back they came, all Tibbut's team except the goalkeeper advancing into Sugden's half, making the pitch look as unbalanced as the 6:1 domino.

But still Sugden held them, held them by threatening his own players into desperate heroics. But it had to come. It must.

12.25 p.m. 26. 27. Every time Billy saved a shot he looked heartbroken. Every time he cleared the ball, he cleared it blind, giving the other side a fifty-fifty chance of possession, and every time they gained possession, Sugden threatened him with violence, while at the same time keeping his eyes on the ball and moving out to check the next advance. So that a sudden spectator would have been surprised to see Sugden rushing forward and apparently intimidating the boy on the ball.

For one shot, coming straight to him, Billy dived, but the ball hit his legs and ricocheted round the post. Corner! Well saved, Casper. No joke. No laughter.

It was a good corner, the ball dropping close to the penalty spot. A shot—blocked, a tackle, a scramble, falling, fouling, *whoosh*, Sugden shifted it out. '*Out*. Get out! Get up that field!'

Billy scraped a lump of mud up and unconsciously began to mould it in his fist, elongating it to a sausage, then rolling it to a dumpling, picking pellets from it and flicking them with his thumb, until nothing remained but a few drying flakes on his crusty palm. He scraped another lump up and began again; rolling, moulding, flicking, then he pivoted and wanged it across the goal at the posts. Flop. It stuck, and when the next shot came towards him he dived flamboyantly and made an elaborate pretence to save it, but the ball bounced over his arms and rolled slowly into the net.

Goal!

Tibbut's team immediately abandoned the pitch and raced across the field, arms flying, cheering. Billy raced after them without even bothering to pick the ball out of the net, or look at his own team, or at Mr Sugden.

He was slipping his jacket on when Sugden entered the

changing room. Sugden watched him, then, as Billy headed for the door he stepped across and blocked his path.

'In a hurry, Casper?'

Yes, sir, I've to get home.'

'Really?'

'Yes, sir.'

'Haven't you forgotten something?'

Billy looked back at the bare peg and the space beneath it.

'No, sir.'

'Are you sure?'

Billy inspected himself, then looked up into Sugden's face.

'Yes, sir.'

Sugden smiled at him. Stalemate. Billy looked past him, and by transferring his weight from foot to foot was able to see the door, one eyed, round each side of him. Right eye, left eye. Right eye, left.

'What about the showers?'

He nodded over Billy's head towards the steam clouding above the partition wall at the far end of the room. Billy stopped rocking.

'I've had one, sir.'

Sugden back-handed him hard across the cheek, swinging his face, and knocking him back into an avenue of clothing.

'Liar!'

'I have, sir! I was first through! Ask anybody.'

He stroked his cheek, his eyes brimming.

'Right, I will.'

Sugden whipped his whistle out of his tracksuit bottoms and blew a long shrill blast, which was still echoing long after the boys had come to order, and for a few seconds produced a ringing silence of its own which was audible even above the hiss of the showers, and the gurgle at the grate.

'Put your hands up if you saw Casper have a shower.'

No hands. No replies. The boys continued their activities quietly. Some were dressing, tousle-haired. Some were drying themselves on the terrace of stone tiles set before the showers. The rest, who had crowded to both ends of the partition wall, drifted back behind it and continued their shower. One boy posed Eros-like, and allowed a jet of water to play into his palm and waterfall out on to the tiles of the drying area. Most of these tiles were varnished with water, their slippery surfaces a-jiggle with the movements of the boys and the refractions from the strip lights in the ceiling. Under the walls a few tiles remained dry, their grey matt surfaces insensitive to this movement and light.

'Well, Casper, I thought anybody would tell me?' Pause. 'Purdey, did you see him under the showers?'

'No, sir.'

'Ellis?'

'I didn't see him, sir.'

'Tibbut?'

He shook his head without even bothering to look up from drying between his toes.

'Do you want me to ask anybody else, Casper? You lying rat!'

'My mam says I haven't to have a shower, sir. I've got a cold.'

'Let's see your note then.'

Smiling, he held his hand out. Billy produced nothing to place in it.

'I haven't got one, sir.'

'Well, get undressed then.'

'I can bring one this afternoon though.'

'That's no good, lad, I want one now. You know the school rule, don't you? Any boy wishing to be excused Physical Education or showers must, *at the time* of the lesson, produce a sealed letter of explanation signed by one of his parents or legal guardian.'

'Oh, go on, sir, I've to get home.'

'You can get home, Casper.'

'Can I, sir?'

His face brightened and he started to move round Sugden towards the door. Sugden performed a little chassé, and reproduced their former positions.

'As soon as you've had a shower.'

'I've no towel, sir.'

'Borrow one.'

'Nobody'll lend me one.'

'Well you'll have to drip-dry then, won't you?'

He thought this was funny. Billy didn't. So Sugden looked round for a more appreciative audience. But no one was listening. They faced up for a few more seconds, then Billy turned back to his peg. He undressed quickly, bending his pumps free of his heels and sliding them off without untying the laces. When he stood up the black soles of his socks stamped damp imprints on the dry floor, which developed into a haphazard set of footprints when he removed his socks and stepped around pulling his jeans down. His ankles and heels were ingrained with ancient dirt which seemed to belong to the pigmentation of his skin. His left leg sported a mud stripe, and both his knees were encrusted. The surfaces of these mobile crusts were hair-lined, and with every flexion of the knee these lines opened into frown-like furrows.

For an instant, as he hurried into the showers, with one leg angled in running, with his dirty legs and huge rib cage moulding the skin of his white body, with his hollow cheek in profile, and the sabre of shadow emanating from the eye-hole, just for a moment he resembled an old print of a child hurrying towards the final solution.

The hot water made him gasp as though it was cold. He stood on tiptoes and raised his arms against it, the hairs on his forearms pulling the skin up to goose pimples.

The nozzles, sprouting from parallel pipes, were arranged in a zigzag pattern so that each one sprouted into the space between two nozzles on the opposite wall. Billy backed into the corner, his arms pressed at right angles against the adjoining walls, trying to outdistance the range of the end nozzle. Then, after a glance to map his driest route, he darted through, ducking and skidding, bouncing from wall to wall, creeping under the walls, looking up at the nozzles and twisting away from their flow into the next one, out of it, under it, through it, his feet slicing the sheet of ground water into bow waves as he crashed through to the other end. Sugden was waiting for him as he turned the corner to come out.

'In a hurry, Casper?'

He closed the gap with his body as Billy tried to squeeze past him.

'What's the rush, lad?'

'Can I come out, sir?'

He considered, while the end nozzle was playing on Billy's back and the back of his head.

'You're not going anywhere till you've got all that mud off and had a proper wash.'

Billy turned back into the showers and began to scour himself with his hands. The mud on his legs had blackened, and was being eroded by the incessant raining and streaming down his thighs. Rivulets of mud coursed from his knees, down the ridges of the tibia to the tiles, to be swept away and replenished with a gush as Billy swept his hands over his knees, and the mud stained his shins, and the tiles, to be swept away, to the gutter, to the grate.

While he worked on his ankles and heels Sugden stationed three boys at one end of the showers and moved to the other end, where the controls fed into the pipes on the wall. The wheel controlling the issue was set on a short stem, and divided into eight petal-shaped segments. A thermometer was fixed to the junction of the hot and cold water pipes, its dial sliced red up to 109 F, and directly below the thermometer was a chrome lever on a round chrome base, stamped HOT, WARM, COLD. The blunt arrow was pointing to HOT. Sugden swung it back over WARM to COLD. For a few seconds there was no visible change in the temperature, and the red slice held steady, still dominating the dial. Then it began to recede, slowly at first. Then swiftly, its share of the face diminishing rapidly.

The cold water made Billy gasp. He held out his hands as though testing for rain, then ran for the end. The three guards barred the exit.

'Hey up, shift! Let me out, you rotten dogs!'

They held him easily so he swished back to the other end, yelling all the way along. Sugden pushed him in the chest as he clung his way round the corner.

'Got a sweat on, Casper?'

'Let me out, sir. Let me come.'

'I thought you'd like a cooler after your exertions in goal.'

'I'm frozen!'

'Really?'

'Gi' o'er, sir! It's not right!'

'And was it right when you let the last goal in?'

'I couldn't help it!'

'Rubbish, lad.'

Billy tried another rush. Sugden repelled it, so he tried the other end again. Every time he tried to escape the three boys bounced him back, stinging him with their snapping towels as he retreated. He tried manoeuvring the nozzles, but whichever way he twisted them the water still found him out. Until finally he gave up, and stood amongst them, tolerating the freezing spray in silence.

When Billy stopped yelling the other boys stopped laughing, and when time passed and no more was heard from him, their conversations began to peter out, and attention gradually focused on the showers. Until only a trio was left shouting into each other's faces, unaware that the volume of noise in the room had dropped. Suddenly they stopped, looked round embarrassed, then looked towards the showers with the rest of the boys.

The cold water had cooled the air, the steam had vanished, and the only sound that came from the showers was the beat of water behind the partition; a mesmeric beat which slowly drew the boys together on the drying area.

The boy guards began to look uneasy, and they looked across to their captain.

'Can we let him out now, sir?'

'No!'

'He'll get pneumonia.'

'I don't care what he gets, I'll show him! If he thinks I'm running my blood to water for ninety minutes, and then having the game deliberately thrown away at the last minute, he's another think coming!'

There were signs of unrest and much muttering amongst the crowd.

'He's had enough, sir.'

'It was only a game.'

'Let him go.'

'Shut up, you lot, and get out!'

Nobody moved. They continued to stare at the partition wall as though a film was being projected on to its tiled surface.

Then Billy appeared over the top of it, hands, head and shoulders, climbing rapidly. A great roar arose, as though Punch had appeared above them hugging his giant cosh. Sugden saw him.

'Get down, Casper!'

Billy straddled the wall and got down, on the dry side. There was laughing—(and gnashing of teeth). The three guards deserted their posts. Sugden turned the showers off, and the crowd dispersed. Billy planed the standing droplets off his body and limbs with his palms, then hurried to his peg and dabbed himself with his shorts. His shirt stuck and ruttled down his back when he pulled it on, and the damp seeped through the light grey flannel, staining it charcoal.

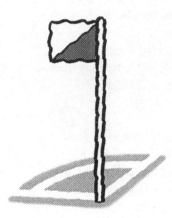

Football Mad

Gizza go of yer footie,
just one belt of the ball?
Lend yer me scarf on Satdee
for just one boot at the wall?

Give yer a poster of Gazza
for one tiny kick with me right?
Do y' after be that mingey?
Go on, don't be tight!

A chest-it-down to me left foot,
a touch, a header, a dribble?
A shot between the goalie's legs,
a pass right down the middle?

Y' can borree me Madonna records
for as long as ever y' like,
I'll give yer a go around the block
on me brandnew mountain bike.

One day I'll be playin' for Liverpule
wen yooze are all forgot:
go on, a titchy kick of yer footie,
one meezly penulty shot?

I'll get yer a season ticket
wen I am in The Team
and wen I'm scorin' in the Cup
you'll be sittin' by the Queen.

Matt Simpson

Away Game

HANNAH COLE

Mr Crendon picked Shazia and Paula for the team.

'My dad would have killed me if I hadn't been picked,' said Paula. 'He didn't want to buy me these boots.'

They were practising ball control in the playground.

'Mr Crendon likes to have his teams winning,' said Shazia, 'so he had to choose the best players, even if he didn't really want us. Haven't you seen him at assembly, when Miss Heyford asks him to read out the results? He looks as though he'd scored all the goals himself, instead of just shouting at the kids if they don't play well.'

'He's so unfair, though,' said Paula. 'He was talking about bringing one of us off at half-time, to give the substitute a chance. Why should it be us that comes off, and not one of the others?'

'He's just old-fashioned,' said Shazia. 'He doesn't think girls can be serious players. But at least he's given us a chance. I wish he'd put me further forward, though. People notice you more if you score. Even if someone is brilliant in defence, nobody notices them.'

'My dad is just the same as him,' Paula went on.

'He thinks it's a joke, me playing football, even though it was him that taught me to play when I was little. He won't even bother coming to watch the match.'

'Maybe Jackie will bring Lucy,' said Shazia. 'She likes giving her new experiences, doesn't she? Like when they came to the harvest service, and Lucy sang "Combine harvester" at the top of her voice when we were supposed to be singing "Kumbayah"—don't you remember?'

Paula was not going to be cheered up. At first she had thought that being picked for the team would be wonderful, but it still seemed that they weren't counted as real players. Mr Crendon had told them that the playing fields, where the match against the Our Blessed Lady of Brieve Middle School would be held, would have no changing facilities for girls, so Paula and Shazia had to go already changed into shorts and shirts.

'What does it matter?' asked Shazia. 'If you're cold you can wear your coat over the top.'

'He was threatening us as well,' said Paula. 'He was looking over our way when he said that he might have to rearrange the team if we didn't do well. He meant, if we don't play three times as well as all the rest, he'll chuck us out.'

Shazia shrugged her shoulders. 'I suppose it's just as bad for a boy who wants to do a girls' subject, like cooking.'

'No,' said Paula. 'They just call him a chef and pay him double.'

Montaz called them over to practise with the rest of the team. Everyone was excited about the match.

'It's a bad start, an away match,' said Anthony. 'The other side will have loads of supporters cheering them on, and we'll be all on our own.'

'Mrs Heyford said she might come and watch,' said Brendan. 'Anyway, it's not as though it's miles away. Most of our parents will be there, and my Uncle Perry's coming. He can shout loud. You should hear him at some of those Oxford matches. He drowns out the rest of the crowd.'

'We'd better make sure all our families do come,' said Montaz. 'You've got loads of uncles,' he said to Shazia. 'Can't you get them to come and shout for us?'

'They might,' said Shazia. 'I don't know, though. They don't really approve. I'll ask my aunt to come. She starts work early in the morning, and she would be free by half-past four.'

Paula said nothing. She had told Dad and Jackie about the match, but Dad had said, 'Half-past four? Do you want to get me sacked, walking out of work early?' and Jackie had said something about Lucy having a rest after her gymnastics, and grumbled about Paula being late home from school.

Mr Crendon drove the team to the playing field in the school minibus. Shazia and Paula sat at the back. They felt a bit silly wearing their shorts and shirts already, while all the boys were in their school clothes. They wrapped their coats round their knees to keep warm. It was an old minibus and the wind whistled in through the cracks round the dented back door. Mr Crendon drove too fast and they were all jolted about on the hard seats. Everyone shouted as they swerved round a corner.

'I hope it's not far now,' said Shazia, 'or my aunt will never find her way here.'

Mr Crendon swung the van up on to the pavement and screeched on the brakes. On the other side of the railings were the playing fields. The Our Blessed Lady team were already there in their orange and white kit. They were sponsored by the chair factory round the corner and had the name of the firm on their backs.

'I wish we had a proper team strip,' said Shazia. 'It looks a lot better than just odd shirts and scrappy shorts.'

At least Paula had the right colour shorts, blue, just by chance, but Anthony and Brendan's shorts were black, and Richard's were green. Paula looked at the Our Blessed Lady team. They looked very big.

'Are they older than us?' she asked Mr Crendon as she climbed down out of the minibus. It was windy and her legs were frozen.

Mr Crendon looked at her scornfully. 'If you're feeling like that already, you'd better say so now and let the substitute play,' he said.

'I didn't say I was scared of them,' said Paula indignantly, but Mr Crendon had walked past her to greet the teacher from the other school. It was a woman teacher, and she shook Mr Crendon's hand with a friendly smile.

'She doesn't know that he's an enemy to girls,' Shazia whispered to Paula.

The boys had run to the changing rooms to get their odd shirts and shorts on. Paula and Shazia warmed up around the edge of the pitch. When the boys came out, Mr Crendon blew his whistle and gave them a talk about watching the ball and looking for people to pass to, not trying to be the star of the match but being one of a team, making spaces for the ball to be passed into, and about the pitch being bigger than they were used to so they must not wear themselves out running up and down it. Paula thought that it was quite good advice, but not the sort of advice that Mr Crendon would take himself.

'You forgot the girls, sir,' Anthony called out. 'Tell them the goal's that square thing down at the end of the pitch, and you're supposed to kick the ball, not pick it up and throw it.'

Mr Crendon pretended not to hear. Some of the boys laughed. Paula wanted to kill Anthony, and she was wondering whether to grab him round the neck, or to kick him to death with her new football boots, when Montaz said, 'Shut up, Anthony. They know more about football than you do.'

Brendan said, 'I'll bet you Shazia could beat you on penalties.'

And Richard Tackley said, 'If you upset the girls and make them drop out, then you'll have to bring the substitute on, and you know I'm nowhere near as good as them.'

Paula and Shazia looked at each other, with their eyes wide open. They knew themselves that they were good, but it was the first time anyone else had said anything better than, 'Not bad for girls.'

The other teacher was refereeing the first half of the match. Her long hair was flying up in the wind like seaweed under water. She blew her whistle for the players to take their positions. Paula looked at the boy playing against her. He was taller than her, and he looked very smart in the orange shirt. He had a nice wide face that looked like the sun.

'Hello,' he said. 'Is this the first match your team has played this season?'

'Yes,' said Paula. 'And it's the first match I've ever played in.'

'I was only a substitute last year,' said the boy. 'What's your name? I'm Alison.'

'Are you a girl?' Paula asked in disbelief. 'I thought Shazia and I were the only ones.'

The girl laughed. She still looked quite like a boy.

'Have you got other girls in your team?' asked Paula. She looked round. The teachers were looking at their watches and talking. She saw that one of the players in orange had long fair plaits down her back. And there was a plump one with a fringe who must be a girl, too. It was strange that they had all looked like boys when she first glanced at them.

'There are six of us usually,' said Alison. 'But two of the girls are off with flu at the moment. There are some boys ill as well. We only just managed to get a team together today.'

The teacher blew her whistle and, as the ball hurtled down to the far end of the pitch, Paula heard Shazia call to her. She looked over. Shazia was pointing to the side-line.

'Keep your eye on the ball!' Mr Crendon was yelling.

Paula looked over to where Shazia pointed. There were a lot of grown-ups standing on the side-line, and some of the Our Blessed Lady schoolchildren had stayed on after school to cheer on their team. Among the crowd Paula could see two of Shazia's aunts and an uncle, and three little cousins.

Paula glanced back to see whether the ball was near enough to worry about. It was still near the other goal.

She looked back at the crowd of supporters. Shazia's cousins and some other little children were screaming, 'One, two, three, four, who d'you think we're shouting for, Oxford United!'

Paula saw them put their heads together to plan their next chant. Suddenly a mob of players tangled their way down the pitch as the ball came down to Paula's end. All of the Our Blessed Lady team wanted a shot at goal, and none of them wanted to pass the ball. Alison ran backwards, hoping for a pass. Paula got ready to stop the ball if it did come their way.

Mr Crendon was screaming to his team to spread out. The other teacher could not shout at her team because she was being the referee, and must not help one side more than the other. But the parents and big brothers and sisters on the side-lines were all yelling advice. Paula noticed that Brendan, who was the goalkeeper, had come out of goal and was hopping around the mass of people, impatient to get a kick at the ball.

In the crowd nobody could see where the ball was going. It suddenly shot out and Alison was ready to take a good shot at goal. Brendan had no time to get back in goal, and it was left undefended. Quickly Paula raced for the ball and with her right foot, which was not her best one, managed to get in just before Alison and kicked it up to the other end of the pitch.

Alison had been swinging her leg ready to kick the ball, and she could not stop in time. Her foot met Paula's leg and they fell in a tangle on the muddy grass. But the ball had got clear. With all of the Our Blessed Lady team up at this end, there was no one to stop it going clear down to the other goal. Shazia passed it on to Montaz, and he was able to knock it in easily. The boy in goal made a good effort at saving it, but it all happened too quickly for him. He dived to the side, but the ball sailed in above him. Perhaps he had hit his head on the post. He leant against it looking rather giddy.

The referee blew the whistle, one–nil. Paula and Alison stood up stickily and looked at the black mud on their shorts and legs. Paula thought she should have some bruises as well, but the mud could be covering them up. She was certainly not going to make a fuss about them, the way that Brendan would have done, rolling about on the ground and pretending that his leg was broken. As the players trotted back to their positions, the referee pointed to Paula and nodded. 'Good play,' she called. Paula was glad that someone had noticed, even if Mr Crendon was only interested in the ball going into the goal, and not how it had got down that end.

Suddenly Paula heard another scream from the little children on the side-line.

'One, two, three, four, which team do we want to score?'

The answer was a mixed scream, but Paula thought she could hear her own name, 'Paula!' and Shazia's as well. She looked over and was amazed to see that it was Lucy standing shouting with Shazia's cousins. Paula glanced back at the pitch, then looked round again to see Jackie standing next to Shazia's aunts. She had to look twice to be sure. One of the aunts was waving her arms; perhaps they were discussing tactics. Jackie was huddled in her big quilted coat, with her hands pushed down into her pockets. She was listening and nodding.

Lucy and Shazia's cousins had linked arms, and they were stamping their feet and shouting, 'Oxford United!'

'Which side do those kids think they are on?' asked Alison.

'They're supporting us,' said Paula. She laughed. Lucy looked so nice, all wrapped up in her coat and mittens, with her scarf tied twice round her neck and her naughty little eyes shining out above it. 'That one with the clothes-pegs in her hair, she's my little sister,' Paula told Alison. 'I'm planning to train her up to be a real footballer.'

At half-time the score was still one–nil and Mr Crendon called the team together to say the same sort of things as he had said before the game started. Paula thought he might have praised the people who had made the goal, but he was just complaining that one goal was not enough.

'It's much too easy to relax once you are in the lead,' he said. 'You've got to keep on pushing at them and really get them on the run. You should be able to smash them easily; they are only a bunch of girls.'

Paula felt her face getting hot. How dare he say that girls were no good! She looked across at Shazia, and felt quite indignant when she saw that Shazia was smiling calmly.

'I think there are some refreshments over by the changing rooms,' said Mr Crendon. 'Any questions?'

Shazia raised her hand. Mr Crendon twitched his eyebrows at her. He did not waste energy.

'Don't you think they could have smashed us quite easily in the first half,' Shazia asked, 'if it hadn't been for the girls in our team?'

Mr Crendon tossed his head and started walking towards the changing rooms. 'This is a team game, Shazia,' he said, 'and if you are just looking for individual praise you had better find yourself a different sport.'

'Why should he be allowed to be so mean and rude?' said Paula to Shazia. 'It's disgusting. I'd like to find out what team it is he plays for on Sundays and bribe the referee to send him off after two minutes. I probably wouldn't even need to do any bribing. I expect he's so mean and unfair that he gets sent off anyway for sneakily kicking people and cheating.'

'My uncle says he used to be quite a good player,' said Shazia. 'He used to play for the Blackbird Rovers. I think he's a bit past it now.'

Paula drank her orange squash and frowned around at everyone.

'What are you in a bad mood for now?' asked Lucy, who was standing behind her. 'I thought you would be pleased because our team is winning. Did you see the goal? Wham! Right in the net! Zainum and I have been practising with our scarves rolled up in a ball, but they keep coming undone.'

Paula undid her frown and smiled at Lucy.

'Well done, Paula,' said Jackie. 'You seem to be doing well. I've never watched a football match before. It's quite interesting.'

Now that Paula was standing still, she was feeling cold. The mud had dried on her legs and felt tight and itchy.

'I'm glad you came,' she said. 'I didn't think we would have many people cheering us on.'

'Lucy!' said Jackie. 'What have you done with your scarf? There's mud all down it! Really, I knew I shouldn't have brought you. And look at your tights. Just try to keep on the dry grass. There's no need to go galloping around in the mud.'

'I'm just practising what I learned at gymnastics, Mummy,' said Lucy. She skipped away with Shazia's cousins, and Paula saw her trying to do a handstand and then wiping her muddy hands on her coat.

The two teachers were talking to each other. Mr Crendon waved his hand towards Shazia and Paula, and the teacher from the other school, Miss Whiteham, was nodding.

'Come here, you two,' called Mr Crendon. 'The Our Blessed Lady goalkeeper has had to drop out. He banged his head in the first half and Miss Whiteham is sending him home. They haven't got a substitute, so I've said that they can have one of our girls. We can bring our substitute on instead. Which one do you want, Miss Whiteham?'

'Well, thank you very much,' said Miss Whiteham. 'Which of you is best in goal, do you think?'

'Shazia's easily the best,' said Paula. 'Nearly as good in goal as on the pitch.'

'Fine,' said Miss Whiteham, and Shazia ran down to the goal. She must try to forget that she wanted her own team to win, and do her best to stop them scoring. She was worried that if she should let a goal in, even if she did her best, the other team might not believe that she had really tried to stop it.

The whistle blew and Paula went back to her position.

'You didn't get changed out, then,' said Alison. 'Is that your substitute over there, that boy with the baggy shorts?'

'Yes,' said Paula. 'And your teacher borrowed my friend to play in goal for you, because your goalie banged his head. It's funny to see her on the other side.'

The ball came down the wing and Alison ran backwards to be ready for it. Another girl passed it to her and Alison took a kick at goal. She was too far away to have any chance, Paula thought, but she was surprised what a strong kick it was. Luckily it was too high.

'Miss Whiteham will be pleased that your teacher is refereeing,' said Alison, when the ball was back down the other end. 'She can scream as much as she likes now.'

Suddenly the ball was crossed in from the wing. There was a shot and the ball was in the back of the net before Paula had seen what happened. The score was one–all and Mr Crendon began to look very grim.

While the action was down at the other end of the pitch, Paula glanced quickly over at the spectators. The children were watching Shazia jigging up and down in goal, but Lucy didn't seem to be standing with Shazia's cousins now. After checking that the ball was nowhere near, Paula looked round. Lucy was trying to climb up someone's legs. It was Dad! He was still in his overalls, so he must have come straight from work. If it was that late, it must be nearly time for the final whistle. Paula began to panic. She suddenly wanted to win almost as much as she had wanted to be in the team to begin with.

The ball came spinning down nearly to the goal. Paula raced for it and passed to Richard, but back it came. She felt certain that the Blessed Lady team were going to score again, but she managed to get the ball and suddenly a gap opened up down the wing. There was no one to pass to, so she took the ball down with her, keeping it close by her feet ready for the chance to pass. Then horrible Anthony yelled. He could take a shot from where he was, but Paula did not want to give him the ball.

Why should I give him the chance to score? she thought, and slowed down.

But Shazia, bouncing about in the goal, screamed 'Pass it!' As soon as she had shouted she clapped her hands over her mouth. She should not have given advice to the opposing side. But there was no time to worry about it.

Paula passed the ball. She thought Anthony would score easily, but someone tackled him. It was more of an attack than a tackle, and Anthony went over like a skittle. It was nice to see him lying in the mud, but it spoilt their chances of a goal. No, Mr Crendon had

71

blown the whistle. It was a foul, and he was giving them a penalty. Paula looked over at Shazia. She wanted Shazia to show what a good player she was, but she wanted the goal as well.

Montaz took the penalty. Paula held her breath and would not hope either way. When Shazia saved the goal, Paula found that she was feeling very pleased. A crowd of boys were banging Shazia on the back.

'Hey, Paula!' Lucy called from the side-line. 'You should have told her to let it in! Then we'd have won!'

Paula waved at her and shook her head. She made her way back down to the other end and Mr Crendon blew the whistle, but before the ball had decided which way to go next, the whistle went again for the end of the match.

'Well done,' said Alison. 'That was great. We are quite well matched, aren't we? We've had some terrible games before, where the other side was much too good for us, or so hopeless that it was a waste of time. But this was terrific. I hope we get to play you again.'

Shazia galloped over to them.

'Well saved,' said Alison. 'Thanks for keeping it to a draw.'

'That was a fantastic save,' said Montaz. 'I didn't have a chance. And you were great, Paula. Old Crendon will have to have you both in the team for the next game, and I don't suppose he'll be so keen on substituting either of you at half-time.'

Several other boys went by and shouted, 'Well done.' One–all was a good score for the first match of the season, and an away game as well. And Dad had arrived in time to see that the football boots had been well worth buying.

Shazia and Paula fetched their coats and stood shivering outside the changing rooms while the boys threw their shorts around inside.

'I wonder what Mr Crendon will say when he announces the result in assembly,' said Shazia. 'I am pleased to announce a one–all draw, achieved thanks to my super-skilful tactical substitution.'

'I'm surprised he didn't demand a transfer fee,' said Paula.

'A million pounds?' said Shazia.

'A tube of Smarties more likely,' said Paula, and Shazia chased her all the way to the minibus.

And Here Are the Football Results

Blackburn 3 . . . . . . Half Past 4
Chelsea 4 . . . . After 8
West Ham 2 . . . . . . Jaws 3
Leeds 1 . . . . Famous 5
Newcastle 0 . . . . . . Secret 7
Everton 2 . . . . M1
QPR 1 . . . . QE 2
Bolton 3 . . . . Page 3
Liverpool 6 . . . . . . Seven 11
Man United 1 . . . . . Figure 8

Peter Dixon

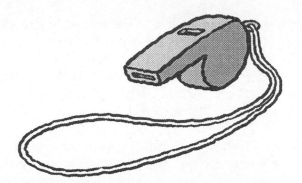

The Match of Death

JAMES RIORDAN

We weren't the best team in the land. Last season we'd come third in the league and reached the Cup semi-finals, losing to Moscow Spartak. Not that I made much of a contribution from the youth team. Still, our coach Ivan Danko always forecast a great future for me:

'Son, you'll make a nifty centre forward one day!'

One day . . .

What day?

The year was 1941. War in Europe had been raging for a couple of years. But Hitler hadn't invaded us. You see, we had a pact: don't fight us and we won't fight you. Surely he'd honour that.

But Hitler didn't believe in fair play. He didn't play to the ref's whistle. Football obviously wasn't his game.

On the night of 21 June 1941 his army crossed our frontier. The Germans were coming. In tanks and planes and black death squads. They mowed down everything in their path.

Soon they were at the gates of Kiev. From our flat on Kreshchanka I watched the tanks rumble through the city—ugly monsters with sinister black crosses on the sides. I hid behind the curtains, while Mum pulled me away.

'Igor, don't even look at Germans—they're vermin, a plague of rats. That's what your dad says.'

Dad had joined the Red Army with my two elder brothers a year back; they'd been holding the line before Kiev. Ahead was the foe, behind were their loved ones. Goodness knows where they were now.

After Kiev's surrender, German signs and swastikas went up on every highway, and helmeted soldiers strutted through the cobblestone streets. Out of the woodwork appeared our own creepy-crawlies, Ukrainians who greeted the Nazis as liberators, who hated Jews and communists, who offered to collaborate.

One such weasel appeared at our door one day. I knew him slightly—Alex Goncharenko, half German. I'd played football with him in the Juniors. Funny that: he was a coward even then, afraid of a hard tackle, yet elbowed you in the face when the ref's back was turned.

Anyway, this fellow barges his way in and says, 'You're to report to the stadium at nine sharp tomorrow! Bring your kit.'

That was all. I was puzzled. The league was wound up at the end of the 1940 season, though we'd played a few friendlies after that—even one against a German side from Dresden. It was supposed to cement German-Soviet relations.

We lost 3–1, though we won the vodka-drinking contest afterwards . . .

Next day I took the tram down to the football ground, arriving just before nine. A German soldier checked my passport and ticked off the name 'Igor Grechko' on his list.

Most of our youth team was already in the changing room, ranged along the wall, staring sullenly at the concrete floor. I was pleased to see my best mate Abram Feldman and I shoved in alongside him. A few of the first team and reserves drifted in. Last to arrive was the Club Coach Ivan Danko and his assistant Oles Ogapov.

Close behind them came a grim-faced German officer and two local 'helpers'. One was the weasel Goncharenko.

With so many bodies crammed into the room, the air was soon thick with cigarette smoke and sweat. It was Danko who addressed us, nervily.

'Sit yourselves down wherever you can, lads. We've been asked to hold a training session for our guests.'

He spoke the word 'guests' like you say 'lovely weather for the time of year' when it's raining cats and dogs. Clearly, as an old-time communist, he hated the Nazis; but somehow he had to protect his 'boys'.

'We'll split into firsts and seconds,' he said.

He started picking the teams.

I was in the seconds, pulling on a light blue shirt with our famous 'D' for Dinamo on the pocket, and white shorts; the firsts were in the customary white shirts and black shorts.

The German kept silent, though the shifty-eyed weasel was whispering in his ear, presumably translating and commenting on each player. Just as we were changing into our kit, the German came over to where I was sitting.

'You, Jew!' he barked. 'Stay put!'

He was pointing a black-gloved hand at Abram.

A deathly quiet descended. Abram was ours, one of our best young players. Until then no one had given any thought to him being Jewish. We had Tatars, Russians, Jews, Ukrainians, even a German in our pre-war squad. But nobody ever saw them as being anything but part of the team.

Coach's rasping voice cut through the silence.

'He plays or no one plays!'

The German glared at Danko, yet stood aside as Abram and I left the changing room together.

Once out on the pitch in the warmth of late August,

we breathed in the fresh smell of grass and bindweed. For a while we could forget the war; we were playing the game we loved.

The stone terraces rang hollowly to our shouts, the goalposts were netless, the blue sky was dotted with grey barrage balloons and dark warplanes. A gaggle of old women with clumps of birch sticks were sweeping the track around the pitch.

We sprinted and leapt in the air, scored goals galore, ran off our nervous energy and puffed and beamed through honest sweat. Abram, our left half, set me up for two goals and I returned the compliment. It was nice to beat our seniors for a change.

After an hour or so Coach blew his whistle and we all trooped off. The showers had no hot water, just a dribble of cold, brackish liquid that hardly wet our heads. We didn't mind.

'Well done, you Constables,' yelled Danko.

Dinamo was known to its fans as 'the Constables'— because the Club was run by the security police.

'Same time tomorrow, comrades, on the dot,' shouted Coach. 'We've a big match on Sunday.'

We wondered what he meant. What 'big match'? Who were we playing?

'Win For Me!'

I went home on the tram with Abram who lived just round the corner, on Lenin Avenue.

'Come and have a glass of tea,' he said. 'I want you to meet someone.'

Like mine, Abram's dad was away in the army. But the cramped flat was full to bursting with little children. There was a sad-eyed skinny lad huddled in the corner; I'd not seen him before. Despite the summer heat, he was shivering.

'This is David,' said Abram. 'He's my cousin; he escaped from Rovno. Go on, tell him, David.'

Words tumbled from the skinny youth like coins from a fairground machine.

'They came for us in the night . . . beat us with rifles, shot the old and sick, even little kids, took us to a football field on the edge of town; then they lined us up and opened fire.

'Mum fell on top of me, covering me with her body. When it was dark I crawled out. Everyone was dead; it was awful.'

He broke down and sobbed as Abram's mother put one arm round him, handing me my tea with the other.

I didn't understand.

'Were you sheltering partisans?' I asked. 'Was it revenge for killing a German? Why should they do that?'

'Because we're Jews,' said Mrs Feldman quietly.

As I walked home, my head was full of unanswered questions. But all my doubts evaporated late that evening. Shouts, groans, curses and the noise of tramping feet rose from the street five stories below. As I rushed to the window, I saw an astonishing sight. Coming down the road was a pitiful column of ragged women, children, and old men. They were flanked by soldiers, bellowing and hitting stragglers with their rifle butts.

For one ridiculous moment it reminded me of a crowd of rival football fans being escorted away after a match. But fans weren't tiny tots in nighties, women with streaming hair, old men on crutches, trying to walk with dignity—and soldiers treating people like animals.

Football fans got more respect.

We turned out the lights so as not to be seen. The column was now passing beneath our block and, all at once, I heard someone call my name.

'Igor, win for me!'

I couldn't see him in the gloom, but I knew the voice.

Win what? The war? I wasn't sure what he meant.

My head was still swimming with the previous night's events when I reported at the stadium next morning. At least half a dozen faces were missing including Abram's. But Coach's calm, if ashen, face gave us comfort. No one dared mention our missing team-mates.

'Right, lads, listen carefully. I don't care who hears since my days are numbered. But I *do* care about you. You are *my* players, *my* team, *my* family. We've a big match on Sunday, the day after tomorrow.'

We all looked at each other, hoping we'd be in the team. Then came the bombshell.

'We're playing a crack Gestapo team from Germany. The Nazis want to demonstrate their superiority. So the idea, dear friends, is for us to lose. If not . . .'

He drew a finger across his throat.

'Win and die, lose and survive . . .' he muttered, half to himself. 'It's a Game of Death.'

We couldn't believe it. Could football be a matter of life and death? For the first time I hoped I wouldn't make the team. And I wasn't disappointed. When the team list went up on the door after training, my name wasn't on it.

Below the team, in small scrawled letters, however, were the names of two subs: Grigorienko and Grechko.

Coach explained, 'The Germans want to allow two subs—maybe they fear we'll break their legs!'

Would my big moment come?

The Match

That day posters went up all over the city.

GERMANY v. KIEV DINAMO
2 p.m. Sunday Dinamo Stadium
Entrance free

80

They need not have worried. Even those who detested football would have given their back teeth to see their side thrash the Germans. Little did the fans know we were going to lose.

'Best of luck, comrades,' said Coach before we took the field. 'I won't see you again—I've served my purpose. Don't let me down: play fairly. And remember: we may not win this battle, but we'll win the war.'

He hugged each of us in turn, tears streaming down his flushed cheeks.

Our captain led us out in our changed strip of blue shirts and white shorts—the Gestapo team wore Germany's black and white colours.

As the German referee walked ahead of both sides on to the pitch, the roar that greeted us lifted our spirits. For the first time that day, it stirred feelings of pride for my country.

I could feel shame later.

For the moment I savoured the sheer joy of seeing and hearing those fifty thousand Kiev fans shouting, *'DI - NA - MO! DI - NA - MO!'*

The thirteen players in each squad lined up in the centre for the national anthems. First came *'Deutschland über Alles'*, which was met in almost total silence. Then, as massed voices got ready to sing the Soviet national anthem, over the loudspeaker came the strains of the pre-war Ukrainian hymn 'The Great Gates of Kiev'.

After a brief moment of surprise, the music was drowned out by full-throated voices belting out our proper anthem:

'So, Comrades, come rally, and the last fight will we face . . .'

There was nothing the Germans could do about it, even though the track was ringed by soldiers pointing their guns at the crowd.

The game kicked off.

I watched from the bench, kicking every ball, making every tackle, heading every cross. Naturally, we were slow on the turn, half-hearted in attack, unwilling to chase and harry. By half-time the Germans were 2–0 up, and the crowd was silent, crushed, unable to comprehend. Now and again, a bold fan whistled disappointment.

There was no Coach in the changing room. Ivan Danko had already been led away to the nearby barracks.

The second half went much like the first, and the fans showed their disgust. No longer did they get behind us, urging us on. Now they were on our backs, telling us what they thought of our efforts.

Midway through the half, our captain limped to the touchline and said, 'Igor, get on and do your best. I'm crocked. I don't care if they shoot me. We can't let our fans down. Better die in hope than live in shame.'

Few of the fans could have heard of me. Yet my appearance on the field was greeted as if I was Dinamo's secret weapon. The game had halted for attention to a German hurt in the tackle with our captain. During the stoppage, our team gathered in our goalmouth, and I related the captain's words.

'We can't let the fans down.'

You only had to look at those haggard, hopeful faces in the crowd to realize what defeat would mean. On the other hand, if we were to win . . .

'Better die in hope than live in shame!'

'Right!' exclaimed Nestor, our goalie, spitting on the ground. 'If any of you cowards want to lose, take my jersey and I'll play out. At least I'll break a few legs before they break me.'

We smiled. No one took up his offer. Coach had ordered us to play fairly. But our mood had changed. When the match restarted we threw ourselves into the game, chased every ball and tackled like terriers. The Germans must have wondered what hit them.

Within five minutes we scored—to the delight of our fans. Fifteen minutes remained for us to draw level. The crowd willed us on, chanted, sang, shouted, swore at the Germans—Thank God the Germans didn't understand Ukrainian!

I hit the post with one pile-driver, headed against the bar when I should have scored, and then shot hopefully from a long way out. As luck would have it, the ball caught the heel of their centre half and was deflected into the corner of the net.

2–2.

The crowd went wild.

My first thought was of Coach. Could he hear the cheering from his cell? I'm sure he could!

With one minute to go the game seemed all over— and our lives were saved. The referee blew his whistle as Nestor was challenged roughly in catching the ball. To everyone's astonishment, the ref was pointing to the spot. Penalty!

Even our opponents seemed embarrassed at this blatant bias.

Amid a cascade of whistles, their captain cooly aimed hard and low for the corner. Yet Nestor took off as if he had springs in his heels, caught the ball and, in one movement, threw it upfield to me.

With no one for support, I raced forward on my own. Three defenders stood between me and the goal. I tapped the ball through one man's legs and tore down the right wing, drawing the second defender. Then I cut inside to take on the other. As they converged in a sandwich from either side, I drew back the ball with my foot, flicked it up and over the defenders, then nipped in between them.

My speed took me through the tackle as they crashed into each other. That left me one-on-one with the goalie.

For a split second I lost my nerve. Then, all at once, Abram's words flashed through my brain: 'Win for me!'

'I will, Abram, I will.'

And I did. The ball flew into the top corner of the net, past the goalkeeper's despairing dive.

It all happened so fast the German referee hadn't had time to blow his whistle for full time. Now he was standing stock still, uncertain what to do. It was only when the German captain placed the ball on the white centre spot that he gave the goal.

The fans danced and sang and cheered as if we had won the war. In a way we had. The Match of Death had turned into the Match of Life for the thousands . . . and the millions.

We could win. We did win. We will win.

Postscript

I'm writing these words from my cell. I'm not afraid to die. I'd do it all over again just to see the happiness on the faces of those fans.

Funny old game, isn't it? Who was it said: 'Football's not a matter of life or death, it's more important than that'?

Can we Have Our Ball Back, Please?

England gave football to the world
Who, now they've got the knack
Play it better than we do
And won't let us have it back.

Gareth Owen

The Goalkeeper's Revenge

BILL NAUGHTON

Sim Dalt had two long, loose arms, spindly legs, a bony face with gleaming brown eyes, and, from the age of twelve, was reckoned to be a bit touched in the head.

Goalkeeping was the main interest in Sim's life. In his nursery days the one indoor pastime that satisfied him was when his mother kicked a rubber ball from the living-room into the kitchen, while Sim stood goal at the middle door. It was rare even then that he let one pass.

He later attended Scuttle Street elementary school, where he was always gnawed with the ferocious wish for four o'clock, when he could dash to the cinder park to play goalie for some team or other. Even in the hot summer days, Sim would cajole a few non-players into a game of football. 'Shoot 'em in, chaps,' he would yell, after lovingly arranging the heaps of jackets for the goalposts, 'the harder the better.'

At twelve he was picked as goalkeeper for his school team. 'If you let any easy 'uns through,' the captain, Bob Thropper, threatened him, 'I'll bust your shins in!'

But he had no need to warn Sim, for it was rare indeed that anyone could get a ball past him.

It was near the end of the season, and Scuttle Street were at the top of the league and in the final for the Mayor's Shield, when a new and very thorough inspector visited the school. He found Sim's scholastic ability to be of such a low order that he directed him at once to Clinic Street special school.

'I suppose you could continue to play for us until the end of the season,' said Mr Speckle, at a meeting of the team, 'and then, at least, you'll be sure of a medal.'

'What, sir!' interposed Bob Thropper. 'A *cracky school* lad play for us? Ee, sir, that *would* be out of order!'

'But what shall we do about a goalkeeper?' asked the teacher.

'Goalkeepers!' snorted Bob. 'I could buy 'em and sell 'em.'

'What,' asked Sim, staring at Bob, 'what do you mean, "buy 'em an' sell 'em"?'

'I mean that they're ten a penny,' grunted Bob, 'especially daft 'uns.' And having made his point he snapped, 'Off with them togs, mate—we want 'em for our next man.' And Sim removed his boots, stockings, and shorts, but when it came to the jersey, he hesitated, but Bob grabbed at it. 'Buy 'em an' sell 'em,' he growled, 'that's me.'

There was a tear close to Sim's eye. 'I'll never buy you,' he hissed, 'but I might *sell* you one day.'

In adapting himself to his new life he was quick enough to grasp any advantage it might offer. He organized games in the schoolyard, and for two years enjoyed some hectic if not polished goalkeeping. And at the age of fifteen, when his mother took him round to different factories for work, he simulated idiocy so as not to be taken on.

'Now stop this shinanikin,' his mother scolded him, 'you're no more barmy than I am. And you know it.'

'You shoulda told the school-inspector that,' remarked Sim.

Every morning, with the 'normal intelligence' boys gaping enviously at him through the factory windows, Sim would set out for the cinder park bouncing and heading a football along the street.

At the age of nineteen he accepted his first job, since it did not interfere with his way of life; also, it had possibilities. It was at Brunt's Amusement Arcade, where the chief attraction was a 'Beat the Goalie' game. There were goal-posts that appeared to be full size, and a real football, and all comers were invited to try to score. It cost threepence for a try, and anyone who scored received sixpence in return. Sim, of course, got the job of goalkeeper.

Maggie Brunt, the owner, was a wizened, red-eyed woman. 'How's it goin', lad?' she would say, giving sly slaps of apparent goodwill on various parts of the goalkeeper's person. By this cunning form of greeting she had caught out a stream of employees who had been fiddling—having one pocket for Maggie and one for themselves.

She tried it out on Sim, time after time, and never once was there the faintest jingle of metal, until finally she decided that the lad must be simple, if not honest. The fact was that Sim—who did things with singular efficiency when he had to—had constructed a special pocket, copiously insulated with cottonwool, and provided with various sections for different coins. Had Maggie turned him upside-down and shaken him like a pepper-pot she would not have heard the faintest jingle, so expertly was it contrived.

There came a day, after some six thrifty years, when Maggie decided to sell the Arcade—and Sim was able to buy it from her. 'Bless you, lad,' sighed Maggie, 'they say you're gone in the head, but I wish there were more like you.'

'It wouldn't do,' remarked Sim, and not without a touch of regret he removed the cottonwool from his pocket.

Bob Thropper's visit to the Arcade was the start of a remarkably prosperous boom for Sim. Bob was a thickset, darkjowled footballer by this time, and the idol of the Hummerton crowd. His tremendous kicking power had broken many goal-nets, winded or knocked senseless a number of goalkeepers, and on one occasion, it was said, had actually smashed a crossbar.

One night, just after a cup-tie victory, Bob and his team-mates, merry though not drunk, were passing the Arcade, when one suggested having some sport with Sim.

'Skipper,' whispered Stan Mead, 'you smash one in!'

Stan Mead dived into his pocket for threepence, when Sim called out, 'Like to make it pounds instead of pence?'

The challenge was taken up at once, and in a moment eleven pound notes were flung down, and Sim covered these with as many out of his pocket. Then Bob Thropper drew back, took his short, confident run, and let go one of his famous drives. Sim was up like a flash, and brought it down with stylish assurance.

Then with a casual air he threw the ball back. 'Are you covering the twenty-two quid?' he asked.

The money was covered in two minutes. 'What about waiting till somebody nips off for your football boots?' asked Stan Mead.

Bob shook his head. 'I could lick this loon,' he snorted, 'in my bare feet'—and with that he took a second shot. It was good—but not good enough. Sim leapt and caught it on his chest. Bob's face went darker than ever. 'Fetch my boots,' he hissed at Stan Mead, 'an' I'll smash him to bits.'

A huge crowd swayed the Arcade when Bob Thropper prepared to make the third attempt. The forty-four pounds had been covered, so that there was a pile of pound notes on an orange box, with a brick on top of them. After having his boots tied up, Bob Thropper removed his jacket, took off his collar and tie, and nodded to Stan Mead to place the ball. The crowd went silent as he took the short run, and then kicked.

The ball flashed forward—it went like lightning, a knee-high shot. *'Goal!'* yelled a voice from behind. But a long thin figure whizzed through the air. There was a thud, the figure dropped to the ground. Nobody could be sure what had happened—until Sim stood up. His face was white. But he had the ball clutched against his heart. Slowly he went towards the orange box and picked up the money. 'Closing time!' he whispered in a low, clear voice. The crowd set up a sudden cheer—volley after volley.

From that night on Sim Dalt became famous as 'The goalie Bob Thropper could never beat!' The Arcade flourished. Sim got offers from many teams, including one from Hummerton club itself.

'When I join your club,' he told them, 'it'll not be as a goalie.'

And it was not many years before Sim's words came true, for there came a chance for him to buy a considerable portion of club shares, and he was voted a director.

One September morning early in the season he was taken round and introduced to all the players.

'Meet Bob Thropper,' said the co-director, 'our most famous centre-forward.'

Sim looked at the man before him. 'Centre-forwards,' he remarked significantly, 'I can buy 'em an' sell 'em—or,' he added, 'I can at least sell 'em.'

Some vague and long-forgotten moment of memory was evoked in Bob Thropper at these words.

He stood there frowning. Then, as Stan Mead nudged him and spoke, it all came back to him clearly.

'Bob, you'd better be looking for a nice pub to retire to,' Stan whispered feelingly, 'because this chap means it.'

Fair Game!

Clear off! You're not playing!
This game's not for you!
Why've you stuck your nose in here?
No one asked you to.

Your legs are thin as tent-pegs,
Couldn't kick a cat!
Can't you see your face don't fit?
Sorry, but that's that!

Cool it! Keep your hair on!
You're too late, anyway—
Samantha picked her team last night,
I picked mine today.

Y'what! You're playing for Sammy!
She wants you on the wing!
But she's the one who said: 'NO BOYS!
BOYS WRECK EVERYTHING!'

So! Sammy's switched the rules, then!
Two can play at that—
Look, *please*, *please* join our side instead,
They're a bunch of *tat*!

I swear I would've picked you,
But Sammy's such a cheat . . .
Hey, Sammy! Eat your heart right out!
We've got Pete 'The Feet'!

Gina Wilson

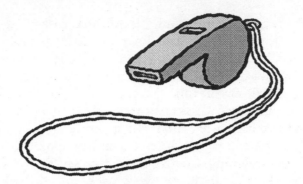

The Kick-Off

DAVE WARD

Len lunged in for the tackle just a fraction too late, just a fraction too high—and that's what started it all, that's what kicked it all off. He'd got carried away in the heat of the fray. He'd meant no harm: no spite, no malice, nothing sly. But he'd hurt the Ellis Street captain's pride. Now the rest of his side were after him: Len would have to pay.

A few moments later Len was up-ended, stud marks on his leg, but the ref didn't see and waved play on. Len staggered up, back on to his feet, just trying to stay out of the way. But his mates had seen what happened: by now tempers were running high. Insults were unbuttoned, fists began to fly. The ref stopped play, lined the culprits up and ordered them off the pitch. At first they refused to go, but when they did the fracas continued on the touchline; trainers and spectators wading in—half urging them on, half trying to prise them apart.

The referee glanced at his watch and blew a long piercing blast on his whistle with over ten minutes to go. Hardly anyone heard it: half the rest of the players had already left the pitch to join in the general mêlée.

Len stood alone and dejected in the middle of the

centre circle, his red and black shirt cascading loose from his shorts nearly down to his bruised and muddied knees. He'd wanted so much to play in this match, Chapel End's crucial game in the Boys' League against local rivals Ellis Street. He'd got his chance when Colin, their regular centre-half, went down with a dose of flu. Len was small but determined: maybe just too determined. He stood now, cuffs flapping over his knuckles, watching as the unseemly scuffle continued off the pitch and all the way back to the makeshift changing rooms.

'It's all my fault,' he muttered. 'That clumsy tackle when I caught him too late—that's what kicked it all off.'

'. . . That's what kicked it all off.'

Len's mother looked at the state of his father as she bathed his bloodied nose, head back in the chair. More punch-drunk than drunk, his words slurred with excitement as he recounted how the Ellis Street men had all been waiting as they tumbled out of the pub. Fathers, uncles, all the cousins of the lads who'd played out that afternoon's match. Some had been there, others had been roped in as the news of the set-to spread through the maze of alleyways that linked the terraced houses and the tenement blocks. They came to settle old scores that had been simmering since they were boys. They came because they'd seen their own boys battling with the Chapel End lot. They came out of honour and excitement to rack out old grudges and hatreds: gunpowder, treason, and plot.

The twilight sky exploded with over-eager fireworks ignited days too early as Len pulled the front door shut behind him and set off down the length of the redbrick terraced street. Every window seemed to watch him as if he were emerging from the players' tunnel and stepping out on to the pitch. He tried to strut, he tried to stride as he reached the alley halfway along: but inside he jittered like a jumping jack as he plunged through the gloom of the lonely back jigger, weaving his way between unlit lamp-posts and overflowing rubbish sacks, zigzagging past packing cases and stagnant puddles.

Ever since the match the air had seemed to crackle like the unexpected bangers, an atmosphere of whispers, rumours, and stares. Catcalls, gestures and a rash of fresh graffiti daubed on backyard walls, marking out territories in the colours of the teams: yellow for Ellis Street and Chapel End's red and black. He could smell the hatred smouldering like early bonfires as the rival gangs from rival streets drew their battle lines.

Len knew it had all kicked off with his tackle, but he didn't know how it would end. He watched it again in his mind like a newsreel and wished he could go back to that moment and run it again. Make the tackle, but make it clean; take the ball from the feet, leave the man and pass it on. Instead . . .

Two shadowy figures dropped in front of him from the top of a backyard wall. Len knew who they were, knew what they wanted.

'We've a score to settle with you, son.'

Len knew that if nothing else he was on his own territory and turned on his heels to run. But with a jarring thud two more figures landed behind him; thickset and heavy they towered over him.

'Think you're clever . . . think you're smart . . . there's two in hospital because of you . . .'

Len knew. He didn't want it. He wished that they weren't there. The push and shove of schoolyard scraps had exploded into the real thing when the men took up cudgels for their sons. But here were their sons come back again, surrounding Len in the alleyway as he tried to make his way to Chapel End's training session.

Faces pushed up close to him. He could taste their sweat, feel their hatred as warning fists jabbed into his ribs. A cry let loose from his lips, at first a shriek of startled fear that turned, as they pummelled him, into a squawk for help, a battle whoop, a rallying call and over the wall from either side scaled elder brothers, cousins too. Mothers and sisters threw in their lot as back gates clattered in response to the racket. Dogs ran barking towards the fray and startled cats flew the other way as the sky lit up again with an illicit rocket.

The four intruders from Ellis Street raced off on heavy booted feet as Len was hoisted shoulder high by Jacob, captain of the Chapel End team, and carried all the way to their practice pitch on the wasteground at the end of the street.

The training session straggled on late into the gathering gloom, half lit by one-eyed crooked street-lamps and punctuated by battle cries, echoed by those from Ellis Street, leering and screeching like wandering jackals out of sight, out of reach three blocks away, yet making their presence felt right there on the pitted, flint strewn pitch that stretched between the walls of two demolished houses on the corner where the grocery shop used to be.

When they finally wrapped it up, they grabbed their coats and fitted the ball snuggly into a duffle bag as they scampered away, taking to walls along the alleyways until they dropped into one deserted backyard and levered up the lock on the outhouse door.

A skeleton frame lurched towards them. Len caught it before it hit the floor. A web of broom handles, old rags and string, a pair of old kecks knotted tight round its waist: only one thing was wanting.

'An Ellis Street shirt.'

An Ellis Street shirt to tie on the guy. This guy to be lighted five nights from now: to burn on the bonfire at the back of the block, with this emblem of hatred in an enemy shirt blazing on the top.

'An Ellis Street shirt for its body and a football for its head.'

Busy hands were already daubing the ball with cartoon eyes and nose and mouth, all in hated shades of Ellis Street yellow, sickly as a bowl of mouldy custard. And on the top where the hair should be a riddle of autographed signatures mapped in their own red and black, spelling out the dread consequences Ellis Street would face if they stepped out of line again.

Eagerly they lashed this football head with lengths of string and sticky tape to the upright broomstick neck, before taking up the cry again:

'An Ellis Street shirt, an Ellis Street shirt,' and snaking out into the night's dark silence to seize one from an unsuspecting washing line, or laundry basket, or maybe even some lad's back if he stumbled lost into their trap.

Len and Samuel set out along the maze of backyard walls, scrabbling over outhouses, hopping on and off pigeon lofts, squinting down into bright-lit back kitchens where blinking faces peered out into the darkness, seeing them but not seeing them as they inched like cats, then bombed in and out like hard-faced starlings.

The closer they crept to Ellis Street, the quicker Len's heart seemed to beat. Tuffets of dandelions grew between cracks, yellow as Ellis Street shirts:

'Wet-the-beds, just smell them too,' as Samuel liked to say.

But now they were no longer so sure of their way, remembering it like a map from previous raids. They peered at the shirts pegged out like flags on straggling washing lines. There were work shirts and best shirts and hand-me-downs. But the Ellis Street team shirts must be all stashed inside, drying in safety on wooden maidens framed around the fire. Everyone knew the

game, everyone knew the annual ritual was to snatch the
other side's shirt as a trophy, yellow or red and black,
and parade it round on their guy before casting it on to
the top of the fire to crackle and gutter and fry.

Another firecracker lit the sky, a fraction too close
for comfort. Len and Samuel dropped from the wall
and scampered back up the alleyway, heading for the
open street and the light where they could thread their
way home at a squinty quick-eyed leisurely lope as if
they'd just been on a message to the late-night corner
shop.

Len and Samuel caught their breath with relief as
they found their feet back on their own territory
where roses were trained around gate-posts, doors
painted red and black and Chapel End team names
adorned the walls. Then they were nearly bowled
over by a whirlwind commotion scurrying up behind
them.

'An Ellis Street shirt. An Ellis Street shirt.'

They caught up the chant as they touched it and
grabbed it, spat on it for luck, as Jacob their captain
and four of his mates hauled the shirt aloft: a captured
flag. As they approached their team's hideout, whooping
with glee, they saw to their horror two silhouettes,
one on either wall, scampering away, dragging the
Chapel End guy between them in the well of the
alleyway.

Len gave out their gang's shrill call as they set out
in pursuit along the wall.

'We've got them now, we've got them now!'—as
they reached a junction at the top. And in their
confusion, one of the Ellis Street lads turned left, and
the other one turned right. The guy's precious frame
was rendered in half, poles and binding splitting under
the strain. Len and Sam grabbed hold of one dangling
pole and hauled its bearer right off the wall. As they
dragged him cursing to the cobbled floor then pinned
him up against a door, far away, and dancing further

out of reach, they caught sight of his accomplice in his yellow shirt prancing away along a wall, their own guy's head—the painted football—hoisted in triumph on top of the pole. He was too far gone now for them to hope to seize it back as he vaulted away like Spring-Heeled Jack, disappearing into the waiting backs all the way to Ellis Street.

Next day Jacob rallied his men.

'Listen, we've got to start all over again. We've got to find a new hiding place. We've got to find a new den.'

They dragged their guy's shattered body between them like a comrade wounded in the war, and propped him up on a dolly tub in Samuel's ma's outhouse. Here they could get to work fixing him, binding the sticks, bandaging his wounds.

Then Jacob held up the Ellis Street shirt, its buttercup colour glinting gold in the pale sunshine squinting through a crack in the high window pane.

'An Ellis Street shirt, an Ellis Street shirt,' they chanted again and again.

'I guess it's one–all. We've got their shirt, they've got our ball.'

'Couldn't we just use another one?' asked Len. 'Just paint it up the same as before?'

'Oh sure,' scoffed Jacob. 'Leather casey balls just grow on trees. No—they took it from us, it's up to us to win it back. We've got to find where they hid it— before Bommie Night. Then we'll have the best guy in the world—an Ellis Street shirt and our ball. Just make sure you keep all *our* shirts safe. We don't want to see them parading red and black on their guy . . . So let's get out there and look for that ball!'

'Sounds like a half-time team talk, Jake.'

'Maybe it is. Like I said, the score's one–all. We've got it all to do. We need wood for our bommie, a head for our guy. And I wouldn't mind figuring out where *their* hideout is after what they did to ours.'

So practice continued every night, running into twilight, balls kicked up and down alleyways, weaving over wasteland, dribbling between lines of rusting cans, broken bricks, and twisted prams till a lofted cross would bounce over a wall, giving the excuse to lift the youngest shoulder high and spy into backyards not explored before to see what they had in the way of wood, cast-out wardrobes, old tables, broken chairs that could be stashed up for the bommie. And most important of all, scanning through windows, testing doors for any sign of the Ellis Street hideout, their guy, or the missing ball.

'We've got to play the match again!' Jacob broke the sudden news. 'The Boys' League Committee have sent a letter to say we're to replay Ellis Street. *And if there's any repeat of the events of last week both teams will be dismissed from the League,*' he quoted from the letter.

'When's it to be?'

'Saturday.'

'*This* Saturday?'

Jacob nodded.

'But that's . . .'

'. . . November the Fifth!'

'There'll be some fireworks then all right. Who've they got to ref it?'

'I hear tell of Father Donnelly.'

'No one had best kick off then. I don't know about getting dismissed, we'll get excommunicated if there's any set-to's.'

'I know—he's been round to see my dad, and he says he's been visiting the Ellis Street lot too. Says he's sick of running up to the hospital visiting men with broken heads.'

Len sat with his own head in his hands, and gazed at the guy that had lost its head and wondered whether they'd all lost theirs as well in the last long crazy week.

'Maybe I'd better not play,' he started to say. 'I'll only get in the way.'

Jacob looked at him, puzzled. 'What makes you say that?'

'All this kick-off. All this barneying. Samuel's dad in hospital. I even hear tell that the Ellis Street captain's uncle has a broken leg. And it's all about me. That's what it is, isn't it? I tackled his nephew . . . that's what kicked it all off.'

Jacob still looked puzzled.

'I don't remember. I do know one of them nearly crippled *you*. That's what got me mad. So then I had a go at their skipper. But I was going to do that anyhow. I'd promised myself that well before the match. I just can't stand him. Can't stand any of that Ellis Street lot. Not just for how they carry on now, walking around like they own the place. No—it goes way back. Some of the things my uncle told me about what they did when *he* was a lad. You think *this* is bad? Wait till November the Fifth.'

'But all the same,' Len pleaded, 'maybe I'd better not play.'

'There's no "better" about it, one way or the other—'

'But Colin's OK. He's been out training—his flu's gone off, just a bit of a cough, and he's always had that anyway.'

Jacob started counting, slowly and deliberately, naming one player for each finger of each hand.

'Ten—we've only got ten fit enough to stand. What with Tommy getting his nose broken at the end of that match and Johnno getting jumped since. He's in no fit state. So you've got no choice about it, Lenny, my lad, you're going to have to play!'

Father Donnelly stood in the middle of the centre circle, his greying hair wreathed like a halo round his head. The touchlines were crowded with spectators, decked out in yellow or black and red. Elder brothers, sisters, uncles; grim-faced mothers with prams festooned in their own team's colours, right down to babies clutching rattles. A stray dog ran yapping across the pitch, not caring which side it was on, just come to rampage with the throng, to find out what all the commotion was about.

Churchwardens, councillors, and Boys' League officials stood in a solemn line, determined to see this match carried off with no blame to be laid on either side. And waiting with them Constable Drew, the local bobby, who was too well aware that the past week's skirmishes had out-run the tactics he usually preferred of a word in the right ear, in the right place, at the right time. In fact, several reinforcements had joined him in the line.

Behind each goalmouth ranged a cluster of older men, subdued and sullen with blackened eyes and arms in slings, or balancing on crutches.

Tension filled the air like the quiet before a thunderstorm, although there wasn't a cloud in the sky. But at each side of the pitch, piled high, stood the rival bonfires of Ellis Street and Chapel End. Grim black structures, silhouetted like the fortresses of the tenement blocks, built out of each street's sadness: discarded furniture and bric-a-brac stacked jagged and cracked, each crowned with the frame of their guy. And each guy proudly wearing a shirt in the colours of their rivals.

Jacob was puzzled where Ellis Street had found their prize. None of the Chapel End players had lost a shirt.

But somebody muttered it must be an old one, hoisted the season before, or longer ago. But the Ellis Street victim was there for all to see. Red faced and embarrassed, his yellow shirt was conspicuously brand new, a different shade too, and with no number on his back.

Until ten minutes before kick-off both teams had paraded their guys up and down behind the spectators on the touchline, accompanied by chants and cheers and cries, until Father Donnelly took matters in hand and ordered them to retreat to their bonfires and leave the effigies there, mounted ceremonially on top.

And now Father Donnelly waited in the centre circle, whistle to his lips. The handshake between the two captains seemed deliberately overdone, each trying to outdo the other with an exaggerated gesture of friendship.

The whistle blew and the game was under way. With Colin back in the side, Len had been switched to the wing. He trotted up and down, trying more than anything to stay out of the way, but drifting further and further in as he became uncomfortably aware that only Ellis Street spectators were lining his side of the pitch. He could hear their raucous comments muttered under breath, and their eyes seemed to stare straight through him even when he was miles from the ball. The Ellis Street captain powered towards him and, rather than risk a tackle, Len fell straight to the floor before his opponent was anywhere near him.

Play stuttered on. Both teams kept making mistakes. Both teams desperately wanted to win, were desperately aware of their relatives' watching eyes, but were just as aware that Constable Drew and all the officials were keeping an eye on them too. No trouble was going to break out again. But everyone knew that watching them all were two rival guys lofted high in the sky. And Chapel End knew, and didn't need telling, that *their* guy was the one still lacking a head.

But as half-time blew with no sign of a score, the missing ball suddenly appeared, still attached to its pole, and was paraded the length of the Ellis Street touchline to taunts and jeers that even the steely eye of Father Donnelly could not manage to stop.

Len recognized its daubed yellow features with the red and black messages picked out on top. He felt an anger rising inside him, felt the urge to whisper to Samuel, 'Come on, let's go and grab it. We'll soon show them all who's boss.'

But then he felt Jacob's hand on his shoulder.

'It's not worth it, lad. Let's play the match. We'll sort out the guys after that.'

So the match ground on as the sun slid down, turning from Ellis Street yellow to Chapel End red, before the black of the waiting dark when the first spark would light the two fires. With one minute to go there was still no score, but the Ellis Street skipper was bearing down on goal. Len came scampering back, trying to catch him. And catch him he did: in almost a replay of his action in the first match, in desperation Len caught him, just a fraction too late, just a fraction too high. And just a fraction inside the penalty box. A sound like a sigh stole round the ground. Father Donnelly paused, whistle to his lips, then finally blew and pointed to the spot.

The faces of the Ellis Street lot were wreathed in mischievous mirth. In an act of defiance to rub in the fact that they were not only about to win this match but the contest of the guys as well, they quickly rolled in their captured ball, smeared in yellow, red and black, and placed it on the penalty spot.

Before Father Donnelly realized, their captain retreated, made his run-up through the soft clinging mud and hit the ball with a dull heavy thud.

The Ellis Street crowd, poised for their victory roar, couldn't believe what they saw as the soft paint-scarred ball floated slowly and harmlessly straight towards

Chapel End's goalie, who gathered it thankfully into his arms.

Then, as Father Donnelly blew for full time, the goalie passed it quickly from hand to hand along a waiting line of Chapel End supporters, back and back till Len found himself standing with it in his hands at the base of the bonfire. Samuel and Jacob hoisted him high as he grappled his way up the tower of wood; and in a string shopping bag thrown to him he lashed the ball to the guy's empty pole. Then from the top of the bonfire he cried to them all, 'An Ellis Street shirt and a Chapel End ball!'

Ms Jones, Football Teacher

Ms Jones,
  football teacher,
red shellsuit,
  flash boots.
She laughs
  as she centres,
shrieks 'GOAL!'
  when she
    shoots!

Ms Jones,
  what a creature,
pink lipstick,
  shin pads.
See there
  on the touchline
lots of
  bug-eyed
    lads.

Ms Jones's
  finest feature,
long blonde hair
  —it's neat.
She back heels
  and bend kicks;
she's fast
  on her
    feet.

Ms Jones,
  football teacher,
told us,
  'Don't give up!'
She made us
  train harder
and we
  won the
    Cup!

Wes Magee

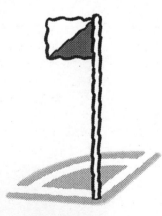

106

The Secret Weapon

SAM JACKSON

'It's 7–6!'

'More like 6–all!'

'Look.' Simon put his hands on his waist and glared at Joanne. 'I'm the one keeping score. We had a penalty, remember?'

Jo flashed him an impish smile.

'Which you *missed*, Si!' She ran a hand through her short black hair and peered at Simon with dark eyes.

'Oh . . . errr,' Simon shrugged as the rest of the lunch-time football crew gathered around. 'But we had another one!' he said excitedly. 'I blasted it past Ryan!'

Jo recalled Simon's stocky frame belting the ball towards goal. Ryan had stood still in the goal, like a Subbuteo figure with his arms poised for a catch. He had stayed still as the ball whisked past his ear, not moving until it had bounced off the mesh fence and walloped him on the back of the head.

Short and cheeky, Ryan was Joanne's best friend, the first year's classroom entertainer. His antics usually had everyone cracking up at least once during the frantic lunch-hour game up on the tennis courts.

'Well, I think we all remember that one,' Jo said

with a chuckle. She gave Ryan a quick dig in the ribs. 'But it's still 6–all, Si.'

Jo sighed. It was the same every lunch-time. About five minutes before the afternoon bell was due to ring out across the courts and playing fields, Simon would become anxious that his team wasn't winning and would try to make out they were one or two up. Jo and Ryan were used to it, but they wished that Simon could just coolly lose the odd game without getting into such a flap. Since he'd been made captain of the first year Sandycliffe High team, he'd become fiercely competitive.

Arguing with Simon was pretty pointless. Jo and Ryan liked to wind him up if they could. His pale blue eyes would grow wide and serious and his shock of ginger hair trembled as he tried to get his point across. Ryan squatted down and began imitating the actions of a large flapping bird about to take off.

Simon ignored him. 'Ask Matt,' he yelled.

Matt Dean was over by the steps on what Jo thought must be his eightieth keep-up, in a world of his own with his precious Adidas ball. Gorgeous Matt Dean, tall and blue-eyed, was Sandycliffe's top goalscorer and master skillsman.

'Hey! David Beckham!' Ryan yelled to him. 'What's the score?'

Matt glanced distractedly towards the group. '6–all.'

Simon threw Matt a murderous look as the others burst out laughing.

'Let's show him,' Ryan said to Jo before jogging off towards his goal.

They started again from the centre. The lunch-time games on the courts were always frantic and Jo's legs were never free of colourful bruises. Simon was good at dishing them out, the way he blundered in at anyone who had possession. But this time Jo nudged the ball left as Simon came thundering towards her. Suddenly Ryan came streaking into the attacking third. Jo touched the ball into his path as he powered through the defence and fired a shot through the middle of the bag markers.

He threw his arms up in an exaggerated celebration. 'Peter Schmeichel eat your heart out! 7–6 to us!'

'Nice one!' Jo told him as they headed in for afternoon lessons.

'Great pass from our lunch-time guest star!' Ryan said, in the style of John Motson. 'If I were captain I'd let you in the school team. You'd easily make it if we picked the best eleven. Simon's such a wally not letting you in. Mr Shaw shouldn't leave it up to him anyway.'

Ryan grinned cheekily. 'You could play up front with Matt,' he said with a wink and proceeded to break into song. 'Because heeeeee's gorgeous!'

Jo shoved him away playfully.

'I'm not bothered really,' she said. 'It's just knowing that Simon and some of the others won't have me in the real team . . . It just makes me more determined. Just one chance is all I want.'

'Mr Shaw said they're mad not to have you,' Ryan said.

Jo stared at him. 'No kidding!'

Simon jogged up alongside them. 'Matt said he made a mistake earlier with the scores so I guess your effort made it seven all.'

Ryan looked at Jo and shook his head. He placed a sympathetic arm around Simon's shoulders and spoke in his ear in low, soothing tones. 'Si, it really is OK to lose the lunch-time game. You're not going to get suspended or anything.'

Simon tutted and walked off towards the science labs.

Jo glanced up at the main block and saw Mr Chambers glaring down at them from the first floor maths room, where she and Ryan were due two minutes ago.

'Oh-oh,' said Ryan. The two of them sprinted to the double doors.

Jo sat in her usual place, next to Nikki at the back of the classroom. Bubbly Nikki Grainger was in trouble almost every lesson for talking and giggling. With Ryan on her other side, Jo wondered whether she should perhaps move if she was to have any hope of getting a half decent maths report this year. It was difficult trying to concentrate on Mr Chambers, standing by the blackboard barking algebra examples, with Nikki whispering ridiculous questions about Matt Dean every ten seconds.

When Mr Chambers began rummaging in his desk Jo turned to her. 'For the millionth time, Nikki. I play footie with the lads at lunch because I enjoy it, not because I want to be near Matt. OK! If you like him so much, why don't you join us?'

'Oh, I couldn't,' Nikki said quickly, fiddling with a long strand of wavy blonde hair. 'I'd be useless.'

Ryan leaned across Jo. 'You're dead right there,' he said flatly.

Nikki lurched at Ryan with her ruler, hitting his hand with several loud slapping noises. Jo wasn't surprised to look up and discover that they had attracted the attention of the stern maths teacher.

Ryan spoke into Jo's ear while trying to wrestle the ruler from Nikki's determined grasp. 'I reckon you should turn up to our practice tomorrow.'

Jo shook her head.

'OK then,' Ryan went on. 'Your netball practice is tonight, yeah?'

Jo turned to him sharply.

Ryan had time to grin and say, 'I'll see you there then,' before his name was bellowed from the front of the classroom.

'Nikki must hold the record for getting sent out of

Chambers's class!' Jo said to her friend Lucy as she finished fastening her red games skirt. 'And Ryan was ordered to sit on the front row with the boffins for the next fortnight.'

Lucy gathered her thick brown hair into a high bunch.

'Why *don't* you go to the practice like Ryan suggested?' she asked Jo. 'The others wouldn't mind.'

Jo sighed. 'I don't reckon they want to be seen to go against Simon, whatever his problem is. He'd really flip if he thought they were all against him.'

Miss Irving handed Jo a net full of orange netballs as the girls passed her on the way out of the PE corridor. 'Be with you in a minute, girls,' she said.

It was ten minutes later when Miss Irving strolled towards the courts, and Ryan was beside her, dressed in tracky bottoms and trainers.

'What on *earth* is he doing?' Lucy spluttered.

Jo eyed the approaching duo suspiciously. She pulled a face. 'I don't think I want to find out.'

'Right, girls!' said Miss Irving as the curious netball squad gathered round. 'We have a new recruit today. I'm not sure whether Ryan has any real intention of representing Sandycliffe at netball . . . But as you know, everyone is welcome to have a go. So, Ryan,' she turned to the surprise guest who was trying to hide an idiotic grin. 'Are you familiar with the rules of the game?'

Ryan smiled confidently. 'Not a clue, miss! But I'm eager to learn.'

'Fine!' Miss Irving looked at him with a slightly glazed expression. Jo felt herself cringing as a giggle rippled around the group. 'Lucy and Jo will fill you in.'

Jo dragged Ryan away from the group.

'You're off your trolley if you think this is going to make me go to footy practice,' she whispered to Ryan sternly.

111

Ryan shrugged, plainly enjoying the stir he was causing.

'Irving was cool about it,' he said cheerfully. 'I should have a laugh, looks easy enough. Like basketball, but duller, yeah?'

Lucy let out a wicked laugh. 'Just you wait,' she said.

Miss Irving handed Ryan the Goal Attack bib for the practice game, and with a glint in her eye promptly organized Deborah Burdett as the opposing Goal Defence to mark him. If there was one person, Jo thought, who *wouldn't* be amused at Ryan turning up it was Deborah—the Simon of the netball crew. Tall and hefty, Deborah towered over Ryan as they stood side by side, poised for the whistle.

From the outset Deborah stuck to Ryan like a giant limpet. Jo watched as his fixed grin slowly settled into an angry grimace as he battled with his marker. Lucy giggled throughout the action. Jo was loving it as well. Seeing her laugh-a-minute friend becoming more furious by the moment was a treat. When Ryan did manage to snatch a pass, Deborah arrived like a giant spider in front of him, waving her arms around to cover any direction he might pass the ball.

Ryan managed one shooting chance after twenty minutes. As he held the ball aloft, sizing up the shot, determination etched on his face, Deborah settled into her defensive stance, balancing on one leg and leaning in like a huge crane to place a broad palm two inches from the ball. Ryan teased her with a mischievous grin and moved the ball from side to side. As Deborah wobbled, Ryan hurled the ball. It crashed against the high fence five yards behind the ring to an outburst of hysterical laughter. It all ended abruptly when the cheeky pretender received a stiff elbow to the chin. Deborah did an expert job at making it look like an accident.

'I have to say,' Ryan said as they walked home, touching his jaw tenderly, 'that was one of the worst half hours of my life. Deborah Burdett is a nightmare. She's possessed!'

Lucy and Jo giggled.

'Like basketball but duller,' said Jo, mocking Ryan's earlier words.

'I'll be back!' he said dramatically.

'Hard luck about not making the team for the game against St Paul's,' Lucy teased.

Ryan turned to Jo.

'But the point is,' he said, sounding like a teacher, 'that if I *had* been good enough, I would have been picked. I made a total dork of myself to show you that you should forget about Simon and his "No Girls" rule and go for it!'

Jo looked at him. 'Thanks for making us all laugh, Ry, but we'll see.'

Thursday's lunch-hour game had been going a few seconds before Jo dodged past a defender to score. Ryan delivered a stinging congratulatory slap on the back. Lucy and Nikki were watching from the steps. Not the football, but Matt Dean. They clapped loudly when he sent a left-footed shot skidding across the concrete past Ryan.

Simon became stressed about the score at the usual time, but even *he* couldn't dream up four goals that didn't exist.

As they piled down the steps at the end of the lunch-hour, Lucy stood up, boldly blocking Simon's path.

'Si, how come you won't let Jo be in the team?' she asked coolly.

Simon smiled awkwardly. The gang gathered round and waited for his response. His cheeks flushed a deep red before he seemed to gather himself and slung his bag over his shoulder.

'Not good for our image,' he said flatly and walked away.

Nikki shouted after him. 'What *image*? We're useless!'

Simon didn't look round.

'He's got a mate who plays for St Paul's, Adam Bennett.' It was Matt who spoke.

Everyone leaned in closer, interested in this new revelation.

'Si said Bennett would never let him forget it if we had a girl playing for us.'

Apart from Lucy blurting her disgust, the news was received with a thoughtful silence.

Nikki gazed up at Matt. 'What do you think?'

Matt paused for a moment. 'I think Jo's good,' he said matter-of-factly. 'I wouldn't mind if I got more service up front.' He shrugged and suddenly, as if sensing the complete attention of the surrounding crowd, he strode away. Nikki almost fell flat on her face in an effort to gather up her bag and follow him.

'So. Simon's scared of looking like a wally in front of his little friend?' Ryan sneered.

'Bennett's totally rubbish!' Parmi said. 'He scored the worst own goal ever that time. He's the guy that always tries those stupid bicycle kicks.'

Ryan burst out laughing. 'No wonder he doesn't want us to get any better!'

Jo looked out across the fields as she headed for the school gates. Down on the bottom pitch the goals had been set out, ready for the evening football practice. Lucy's words during History still echoed around her head.

'The others want you,' Lucy had urged.

Jo sighed. It just wasn't her style to force her way into anything. Simon would have to ask her. Rounding the corner, Jo almost collided with the broad figure of Mr Shaw.

'Sorry, I was miles away,' Jo said apologetically.

'Joining us?' the teacher asked with a broad smile.

Jo shook her head.

'It'll be a tough one on Saturday against St Paul's. I'd love to show that games teacher of theirs we can do something,' Mr Shaw mused.

Jo sat in the shelter on Saturday morning and watched the double-decker bus sail past. Lucy was late again. Jo glanced at her watch. Half-eleven. Sandycliffe would be well into the second half of the game against St Paul's.

Jo looked up when she heard hurried footsteps. Expecting Lucy, she felt a shudder of surprise to see Matt jogging past. He spun round as she called his name. Matt looked stressed, yet he was clearly relieved to see Jo.

'Lifesaver!' he said breathlessly. 'Got to get my kit up to school for Mr Shaw . . . wants to send faulty shirts back after the game . . . '

Jo frowned at him. 'But why aren't you playing?'

Matt swallowed and began to speak more regularly. 'My brother set fire to our living-room, the little pain, just as I was about to set off. Mum thought he was old enough to be left on his own as well. Our neighbour is sitting with him while I take this up to the school, but he's going out so I can't be long. Will you do me a massive favour and take my kit to Mr Shaw?'

Jo took the handle of the heavy black bag.

'They must be playing with ten men,' said Matt. 'Andy couldn't make it either, I just saw him.'

Jo watched him dash away. She looked at her watch again. If she hurried, she would get to Sandycliffe just as the match was ending. An idea was beginning to take shape.

Lucy appeared by the shelter, her hair wild from the wind.

'I've got to get to the school,' Jo said urgently and she began to run.

Five minutes later she was beside Mr Shaw on the touch-line.

'Matt's kit,' she explained. The PE teacher thanked her distractedly, not taking his eyes away from the game. He told Jo the score was 1–0 to St Paul's. The match was nearly over.

'Turning up to play St Paul's with ten men!' Mr Shaw said angrily. 'Their man thinks we're a bunch of fools!'

Jo noticed the smug-looking rival coach.

The action was in the St Paul's penalty box. Jo glanced at Ryan, standing on the edge of his area. His hands in the huge keeper's gloves were frantically beckoning her. It was the last push Jo needed.

She threw away her heavy coat and began rummaging in Matt's bag. She pulled on the white number ten shirt over her plain top and the long, baggy shorts over black leggings. Her own suede trainers would have to do.

Mr Shaw hadn't noticed the frantic activity beside him. His eyes nearly popped out of his head when he turned and saw Jo ready to join the action. Without a word he signalled to the referee. Jo took a last glance around and saw Lucy thudding down the slope.

'Go for it!' she yelled and Jo ran on to the pitch feeling more nervous than she had ever felt in her whole life.

Of all the Sandycliffe team, Simon was the last to see Jo. A look of utter shock swept over his face as she sprinted towards the St Paul's area. Jo stood in front of him, waiting for instructions, but Simon just gawped. He glanced towards a fair-haired boy dressed in the dark red St Paul's strip. The boy was smiling slyly at Simon. Jo realized this must be Adam Bennett.

'Where do you want me?' Jo's shriek seemed to snap Simon out of his trance. 'We . . . we've got a corner,' he stammered, then focused on Jo properly. 'You take it.'

Jo raced to the spot. Ryan had approached the halfway line. He was clapping his hands madly.

'Float one in,' he yelled.

Jo stood five paces back from the ball. 'Please don't let me hoof it behind the goal,' she whispered. As she took powerful strides into the shot, a sudden gust of wind lashed in towards the goal. The ball left Jo's foot with a full, powerful contact—too far behind the waiting Sandycliffe trio of Simon, Parmi, and Dave— until it began to curl in towards the crowd in the box.

Jo stood frozen to the spot. Parmi and Simon rose together towards the floating cross. Sandycliffe's two tallest players drew in the St Paul's defence. But at the last moment, a reverse gust whipped the ball away from its intended target. It passed by the scrambling bunch of players who had launched themselves towards the cross. But suddenly Ryan was there streaking up to the far post to slide the ball past St Paul's sprawling goalkeeper.

Ryan led the charge towards Jo with his usual two-armed celebration and Simon was right behind him.

'Wicked cross!' Simon shrieked.

Ryan and Jo were carried along amid hysterical whoops of delight from the rest of the team. Jo couldn't help noticing the mean stare Adam Bennett was giving Simon.

Ryan nudged him. 'Your mate looks mad,' he said.

But Simon didn't look bothered. 'No wonder,' he said, grinning broadly. 'He doesn't have a secret weapon, does he?'

The last minute went by in a complete whirl for Jo. She watched, dazed, as Bennett legged Simon over in the St Paul's area. The Sandycliffe captain blasted home the free shot to make it two–one to the home side. At the final whistle Mr Shaw looked almost delirious with delight. Lucy gave Jo a massive hug.

The Sandycliffe team walked away from the school still buzzing with excitement.

'Was one go enough, then?' Ryan asked Jo.

Jo looked round at them all. 'For now,' she said, unable to hide a huge grin. 'I can't take this kind of madness every Saturday!'

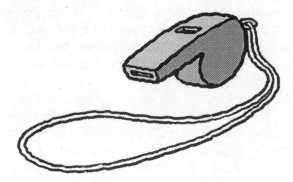

Whisked Off

It was halfway through the second half,
four ahead we were,
and I had notched a hat-trick up
when suddenly in the air . . .

it wasn't a thudding muddy ball
but a shiny metal glob
humming and thrumming and droning . . .
then suddenly this Blob,

greeny-purple, seven heads,
legs like an octopus,
came slithering down a ladder
and asked which one of us

was knocking them in
and who had slammed in three,
we want him to play for Venus, he said.
Me, I said, *that's me!*

That's how I travelled in Outer Space
in a silvery UFO
and how I played for Venus
those many years ago.

And if you don't believe me,
just ask your uncle Roly,
who got whisked off the same as me
and played for them as goalie!

Matt Simpson

Footballers Don't Cry

BRIAN GLANVILLE

The phone went at one in the morning, and I knew who it was. Oh, no, I thought, not him, but it had to be him. We'd only got the baby off an hour ago.

'Peter,' he said, 'I've lost me job.' There were tears in his voice. It was pitiful, honestly. Him. The Iron Man. But I couldn't sound surprised. It had been coming for weeks.

'Called me in tonight and sacked me,' he said, 'the bastards.'

This was what shocked me; his tone. The feeling sorry for himself, after all he'd dinned into me over the years, right from the very beginning. Don't squeal. Pick yourself up and get on with it. Footballers don't cry. Football's a game for men, not lasses. If they kick you, you kick 'em back. All that, and so much more. Never give up. Never to feel sorry for yourself. And now here he was, how they'd done this to him, how they'd done that to him, full of self-pity, wanting comfort, till it was almost like I was him now and he was me.

'Peter,' he said, 'Peter. I hope you'll never know what it's like to have this happen to you. To be stabbed in the back by a lot of fat, ungrateful businessmen that know damm all about this game. That's what hurts. To

120

take it from them; me, that's given my life to the game.'

I was still half asleep. I said, 'Yes, Dad. I know, Dad.' Marion came out of the bedroom, yawning and rubbing her eyes. 'Who is it?' and I said, 'It's Dad. He's just got the push.'

'Not again,' she said. 'It's the middle of the night. You're going to wake John.'

'Dad,' I said, 'I'll phone you in the morning.' I felt bad: I knew he wanted to go on, pouring it all out, and I felt worse, because I knew I didn't want to listen. 'God bless you, Dad,' I said. 'I'll phone first thing tomorrow.' Then I put down the phone and took it off the hook, else I knew he'd be back. It was a terrible thing, that. Little moments, little movements, yet you're changing a whole life.

I didn't sleep. I lay awake, thinking. What he'd done for me, how much I'd always admired him. Just a little lad, going to watch him play, at Bolton and at Rotherham; then later on, when he dropped out of the League, at Wigan and Boston and Kettering. Get in, Dad! Go on, Dad! A centre half, great big fellow, coming in bang with his thick legs, ploughing through the mud with his sliding tackles, taking the man, the ball, the lot; jumping above the centre forward, thump with his head, always first to the ball, a hard man, very tough, very brave, very strong, a bit dirty; though I never thought that, then.

All those little back gardens. Left foot, right foot, left foot. 'Come on, Peter, come on!' I was frightened of him, me. Him so big and me so little. Like mother, never really growing.

'You'll be a winger,' he said, when what I wanted was to be a centre half, like him. Big and strong. Coming in like a tank.

Later, there were all the piddling little jobs he had, coach of this, manager of that, of nothing. Clubs in the Midland League, clubs in the Northern Premier, always in debt, playing in front of the few hundred people; him having to do everything, mark out the pitch, mow the grass, treat the injuries.

'Peter,' he'd say, 'you're my answer, son. When you make it, I'll make it. The war did me, Peter, as a player. Took the best years of my career away. Stopped me realizing my potential. If I'd played for England like I should, there'd have been no stopping me afterwards. Manager of Arsenal, manager of Everton. Look at Matt Busby. Captain of Scotland, end of the war—manager of Manchester United. A great team ready waiting for him. Me, I had to start with rubbish. I've done miracles with rubbish. Worked wonders with rubbish. I knew about recycling before it had ever been invented. But you get no medals for that.'

And he hadn't. He'd last three months here, six months there, then something would snap, he'd quarrel with the chairman, blow his top to the Press, even thump one of the players, and out he'd go, off we'd go; another little house, poor mother packing and unpacking all over again. No wonder she was worn out. No wonder she died.

'But you, Peter,' he'd say, 'you will justify me. By your career. By your skill. By your determination. And then, Peter, they may begin to listen. They will begin to see that I practise what I preach; through my own son, who nobody can say I did not develop.' He'd put his hand on my shoulder, this very emotional look in his eye. 'You'll never disappoint me, Peter: I know that.'

I wouldn't; I knew it too. I'd rather cut my leg off.

I'd never been so chuffed as when he got that job with City. More than when I came to Rovers, and to London. Even more than when I first played for England. And, to be honest, I think I know why. There was relief in it. Not just because he'd be happy now, he'd stop complaining now; but because, in a funny sort of way, things were like they should be again. Me an

England player, but him a top manager. With only one thing spoiling it; for him, not me. Knowing people were whispering and hinting. Would he have ever managed City if he hadn't been my father, if I wasn't playing for England?

Ignorance, that was. 'And why did I play for England?' I'd ask, whenever I got wind of it. 'Because of him; Dad and his coaching.' But you could see by their faces that you'd not convinced them. I couldn't even convince Marion. 'He didn't make you,' she said. 'I'm sick of hearing that; from him and you. He was lucky to have you.'

'No, no,' I said, 'you don't know football, Marion.'

'I know him,' she said, 'and I know you.'

The next morning, when we woke, the first thing she said was, 'He's not coming to stay, is he?'

'I don't know,' I said. 'I've not thought.'

She'd never forgiven him, though I've always told her it was nothing personal, nothing against her, even if he was wrong; just his feelings for me, and my football.

'You mean him and your football,' she'd said.

He'd always told me, 'Don't get married early.' I'd tried to explain it to Marion. 'It's not you,' I said.

'No,' she'd said, 'and it's not you either; it's him, everything for him. He wants you to be a little puppet, dancing to his strings.'

It was a bad time for me, that, pulled one way and then the other. My form suffered. I loved her, I loved him; and I loved football. That was the time I missed a penalty in the semi-final against Leeds at Villa Park, and we went out of the Cup. I didn't see her for a week and I wouldn't talk to him. Then one day I walked into the hairdresser's where she worked and said, 'Come on, I've got the licence,' because it had to be like that: I either had to marry her or give her up, and if I gave her up it would shatter me.

'My mother,' she said, 'my father'; but I told her, 'Never mind them, and never mind my father. I've got two witnesses; we'll have the church wedding later'; and we did. I'd had to do it like that. For the first time in my life, I'd started hating him.

'My own son,' he's said since, 'and I wasn't invited to his wedding.' When we stepped out of that gloomy little registry office, I went straight into the post office along the road and I sent him a telegram: MARION AND I MARRIED TODAY BIGGEST MATCH OF ALL LOVE PETER. We didn't hear from him for ten days, and then he sent a silver teapot that must have cost him a bomb.

'Marion,' he said, when he came over from Hartlepool, where he was coach then, 'I want you to know I've got nothing against you. I never have had; I've always thought you're a wonderful girl, but Peter and me, we've always lived for football, and I'll admit I've been anxious for his career.'

'No more than what I am, Mr Coleman,' she said.

But things changed; it was inevitable. The moment we walked into that registry office, they'd changed; it was the first big thing in my life I'd ever done without him, the first I'd ever done against him. But when he got the City job, that changed things, too; it helped to change them back again. It wasn't me getting two hundred quid a week while he got forty any more, and much too proud to accept anything. Time and again I'd say, 'Look, Dad, it's yours, you did it; I'd be nothing without you.'

'I'll not take a penny,' he'd say. 'The satisfaction I've had from you, you can't buy it.' He's a wonderful man, if you only but know him.

So after breakfast, while Marion was feeding the baby, I telephoned him. He was still in the same state. 'They're being very vindictive about it,' he said. 'There's still nearly eighteen months of my contract to run. Ten grand they owe me, and they've as good as told me I can sue them for it. And this club house; they're turning me out of that, as well.'

'Dad,' I said. What else could I say? 'Come down
and stay with us.'

'You're sure?' he said. 'How about Marion? What
about the baby?'

'There's tons of room, Dad,' I said. 'Marion won't
mind. Just until you get settled. Till you get another
job.'

'For a week, then,' he said. 'But only that, mind.
Just till I get fixed up.'

She was choked when I told her, Marion. 'Without
even asking me,' she said.

'Just for a week,' I told her, 'while he looks around.
He's shattered, Marion.'

'He'll shatter us,' she said.

He was in a state when he got to us. All tense and
taut, that twitch at the left side of his mouth. 'It'll be
down to your knees, soon,' he said, looking at my hair.
His was the short-back-and-sides he'd always had.
'Hello, Marion,' he said. He kissed her on the cheek,
and she took it like it was a vaccination. Then he kissed
John, the baby, and his face relaxed; he liked the baby.
He started playing with his fingers, but he burst out
crying. 'He's tired,' Marion said, and took him away.

The old man glanced around the place. It was a
lovely house; it had cost thirty thousand. Nice, big
rooms, big picture windows, looking out on a golf
course at the back, colour telly. 'By gum,' he said, like
he always did, 'things have changed a bit since I were
playing.' I hoped he wasn't going to come out with the
usual rigmarole, my hair, my hundred-pound suits, my
embroidered shirts, because I knew it by heart: 'What's
that? The Playboy Club? In my day it was eight pound
a week and a pint at the boozer.'

Now he looked out the front and said, 'That your
new car?' It was an XJ Jag. He shook his head; I was
used to that as well. 'I don't know,' he said. I hoped he
wouldn't go on about buses and bicycles.

He sat down on the leather sofa, he slapped himself

on the knees, he gave the laugh he always gives when he's miserable, and he said, 'Well! Now let's wait for the offers to come pouring in!'

'It's early days, Dad,' I said.

'Oh, yes,' he said, 'I don't expect them to come rushing. Not falling over themselves. After all, where did I leave City? Only three places off the bloody bottom. Where will they finish now I've gone? Right at the bottom.'

'Don't feel bitter, Dad,' I told him.

'Bitter?' he said. 'I'm not bitter. I'm resigned to it, me. Directors, bloody amateurs, obstructing a professional.'

'That's the system, Dad,' I said. 'You'll not change it.'

'It's a bloody diabolical system,' he said, and I was afraid he'd be off on another of his favourite moans— directors and how ignorant they were—but instead he went quiet, not even looking at me, sitting there like he was embarrassed, till at last he said, 'You don't think there'd be something for me at Rovers?'

It left me speechless. It was the first time in my life he'd ever asked me for anything. 'Well, Dad,' I said, 'there might be. Not as manager, just now, nor as coach. They go together, do those two; everywhere Geoff Creamer goes, Bobby Birchall goes with him.'

'I know,' he said, 'I didn't mean that,' which made it worse, because what else was there? Scouting? Looking after the Reserves? Those weren't for Dad; they never had been.

'Maybe I could help with the coaching and the scouting,' he said. 'Something like that. Weighing up teams they're going to play.' He looked at me. The look was new as well, almost pleading. What had happened to him?

'I'll try tomorrow,' I said. 'I'll see the boss.' Then I made an excuse and left the room. It was too much for me.

I did talk to the boss, Geoff Creamer, next day. He was uneasy, I could tell he didn't want to upset me. At the same time obviously he knew about Dad, his reputation. 'There's not much for him here, Peter,' he said, 'not for him.'

'Just a bit of scouting and coaching,' I said, 'to be going on with. It's shattered him, this. I think maybe he needs to get his confidence back.'

'I'll talk to the chairman,' he said, and a couple of days later he called me in and told me, 'We've got something for your father, on the lines he asked for. I'm afraid we can't pay him a lot, but if he regards it as a port in a storm . . . '

So he started with them, coaching and scouting like he'd wanted, going to look at teams and players for the boss, taking individual players for special skills, out at Epsom, where we trained, nice and near my home. Of course, I was glad he'd got the job, very glad—for him—but it made things strange. Him being at the club, him living at the house. We'd gone back, and yet, if you see, we hadn't gone back. Dad couldn't change; you couldn't expect him to. He'd still tell me what to do, how to play, when to go to bed, even when to go on the job—'Never the night before a match; it's like losing two pints of blood'—like I was still a kid. Marion could hardly keep quiet if she was there when he did it; she'd wriggle, she'd make faces; I was afraid any moment she'd say something, and afterwards she would. 'I don't know how you put up with it. Treating you like a baby, and he wouldn't have a job if it wasn't for you.'

'I know,' I said. 'That's why I put up with it. He knows it, too. He's on forty-five a week; our reserves earn more than that, but without him what would I be earning?'

But it wasn't easy to get her to see it like that, especially with the baby keeping her up and taking all her time. She said, 'I've heard of mothers-in-law . . . '

Once a day he'd say, 'I must move out. I mustn't burden you. I'll find a room in a hotel.'

'If I hear that once more,' Marion told me, 'I'll go straight out and find one for him.'

I took her hand; she looked very tired. 'I know,' I said. 'I know.'

But I couldn't hurt him, even if it sometimes drove me up the wall, the diagrams, the salt and pepper pots on the table, the 'action replays', as I thought of them, going over and over some move I'd made or hadn't made, like after a game we lost at home to Newcastle.

'The one-two,' he said. 'It was on. It was screaming at you. Even with that big camel of a centre forward of yours. Going through alone: that was daft, but then you always were a greedy little bugger.'

Another time I missed a penalty at Birmingham. That was good for a week, that. My run-up. The way I'd struck the ball. Hitting it high instead of keeping it low. The position of my body. The goalkeeper's position. 'Low and angled, low and angled. How many times do I have to tell you that?'

A million.

Mind, it was only a year ago or so I'd stopped the phone calls, or most of them, the post-mortems we'd have after every big game, even in Europe, especially with England; I remember phoning him once from Caracas, when I really felt I'd played bad. It began to fall off after I got married. Marion would say, 'Phoning your father again?' or 'I suppose you'll be on the phone for an hour tonight.' Perhaps I'd outgrown it, I didn't need it so much now, but she could never realize how it had helped me all those years.

Now and again I'd look at his face when he thought I wasn't and I'd see the bitterness, the disappointment. That was the end, with City—I knew it and he knew it—the end as far as managing a big club was concerned. He'd upset too many people. No wonder he was afraid to leave us, no wonder he was for ever lecturing me; I was all he'd got left.

And then it started at the club. I'd been afraid it would. First he didn't reckon the coach, Bobby Birchall, which was par for the course; he never reckoned any coach, especially one that was coaching me. He'd be out on the field there at Epsom when Bobby was working with us, shaking his head, clicking his tongue, making faces, till it was obvious that Bobby noticed and naturally he didn't like it. There was no future in it either. It was like I'd told him: where Geoff Creamer went, Bobby Birchall went. Geoff Creamer sat in the stadium and handled the directors and the Press, Bobby Birchall was out at Epsom looking after the tactics and the training. If you knocked Bobby, you were getting at Geoff.

One day Geoff had me into the office; he said, 'Peter, you'll have to talk to your father.' I'd been expecting this. 'We're glad to have him here,' he said, 'till he gets something else, but he must realize Bobby Birchall is coach; and I'm the manager.'

'I know,' I said, 'but it's difficult for Dad. He's used to helping me.'

'Just a quiet word,' the boss said. 'I shouldn't like anything to go wrong,' and he gave me what we used to call his Man Management smile, the smile on the face of the tiger.

Of course, I didn't talk to Dad: how could I? He'd no time for Bobby, and even less for the boss. 'They'll burn you out, this club,' he'd say, 'using you like they do. This 4-4-2. They want you on both bloody wings; and fetching and carrying in midfield. I'm going to have a word with Geoff Creamer, if it goes on. You'll not last three seasons. I'll tell him, "You're killing the goose that lays the golden eggs."'

'Please don't, Dad,' I said. 'I can tell him myself.'

'Ay,' he said, 'but you haven't, have you? It's just as well I'm here.'

The trouble was there was truth in what he said, like there nearly always was; they had been working me hard, for a couple of seasons now, and I was beginning to feel it, but it wasn't any good telling them; it would just make it worse. I'd wince, sometimes, when the boss and the old man were together.

'Work rate?' the old man would say. 'What's all this bloody work rate? Footballers aren't factory hands. Footballers aren't navvies.'

And the boss would cock his little head and stick out his little fat arse in the way he had and smile his smile and say, 'Football's changed a lot, you know, Ted.'

'Maybe,' said Dad, 'but it hasn't changed for the bloody better.'

The big blow-up came when we played Milan in the first leg of the European Cupwinners' Cup quarter-final, at our place. Everything went wrong in the first half. They were playing this packed defence with a sweeper, body-checking a lot, shirt-pulling, and when they broke away and scored we got desperate, just banging long balls into the middle, which their defence were eating.

At half-time, Bobby and the boss came into the dressing room with the old man, who'd been sitting on the bench with Bobby—they'd sent him out there to watch Milan. As soon as I saw him I could tell we were in for trouble; I knew that look on his face. He was bursting to bollock everybody in sight and, to make matters worse, the boss and Bobby just stood there like a couple of dummies with nothing to offer at all. I was longing for them to say something, anything, just to fill the silence, before the old man leapt in; which he did.

He started, 'Well, if you two haven't got anything to say, I have. I've never seen such a pathetic exhibition. You're playing right into their hands. No skill, no method, no intelligence.' On and on he went, and whether the other two were too surprised to try and stop him or too chicken I don't know. The fact is they didn't. He bollocked us for using long balls into the middle; he bollocked us, especially me, for not going to the line and pulling the ball back—'You try getting there,' I said, 'with the shirt-pulling and the obstruction'—and he was still at full blast when the buzzer went for the second half. Bobby and the boss hadn't opened their mouths; we left the three of them behind us in the dressing-room, and I wondered what they'd say to one another.

The thing was that his pep talk worked; I think that's what they couldn't forgive him. We did get our tails up; we did start playing better; we did start going round the back of them; we equalized, and very nearly won.

After the match the boss didn't show in the dressing room at all, just Bobby, looking a bit sheepish, and the old man, who of course was just full of it; he never could read situations outside football. 'That was better, lads, that was better. If you'd played like it the whole of the game, you'd have bloody annihilated them!' But all I kept wondering was where the boss was, and what he was saying to the chairman.

There was a reception afterwards, the usual drag, speeches, a cold buffet, and a couple of beers at most, because you knew the boss was looking. He didn't speak to the old man, nor did any of the directors. There was what you might call an atmosphere.

The word went round that a few of the lads were going on to the Sportsman's Club. I asked Dad if he'd like to come, nearly got my head bit off. 'A club? After a game like this? If you'd been trying, you'd all be too tired to do anything but go to bed, which is what you should do, after a match'—another of his favourite moans. So it was a confrontation, the last thing I wanted; the two of us standing there, glaring at each other, but I couldn't back down, not in front of the lads. 'Well, I'm going, Dad,' I said, 'I'll see you later.'

He went on staring for a while and then he said,

'You little tyke,' and walked away. I felt bad leaving him.

We were there till nearly three in the morning, but when I got home the light was still on in the front room. He was sitting there with his head in his hands. I'd never seen him look that shattered, eyes all red; he looked a hundred years old.

'They've sacked me, Peter,' he said, and he began to cry.

'I'm sorry, Dad,' I said, and he said, 'Sorry? Is that all you can say? You're not going to stay there, are you? You'll ask for a transfer?' But I shook my head.

Get up, I thought, get up; footballers don't cry. The words sprang into my throat and choked me. I knew he'd never get up now.

Playing for the School

Looking lively, running out,
yellow strip, boots all shiny with dew.

November morning. Air brisk on cheeks,
on knees. Puffing clouds. Then sir

shrilling his whistle and black rooks
coughing in the sticks of trees.

Booted ball, thudding, slithering
like a greased pig. Ninety minutes'

muscled battling. Mud all over.
Bruised warriors trudging in.

Tired. Winners. Hot as boiled eggs.

Matt Simpson

FA Rules OK

Life isn't easy in our house.
My dad's a referee.
He's always right, never wrong
And he knows all the rules.

Everyday he comes home
Shiny black shirt
Shiny black shorts
Shiny red face
Shiny silver whistle.

He races around the house
Checking the nets on the curtains
The height of the crossbars over the doors.

He doesn't like it
When the budgie talks back to him,
He gets mad when the dog
Dribbles down his leg,
And he booked the cat for spitting.

If we don't wash our hands before tea
That's it—a warning.
Leaving our greens—yellow card.
Giving them to the dog—red card.

Being sent off in your own house
Is no fun.
It's a long lonely walk upstairs
For that early bath
Early bed, no telly
And no extra-time.

Yes, life isn't easy in our house.
Dad's always right
And he knows all the rules.

Paul Cookson and David Harmer

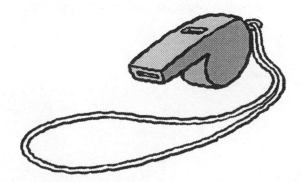

Oh, Please . . .

Oh, please—
let me be in your team,
let mine be the name that you pick,
don't leave me to mope at the edge of the field,
resenting each jump and each kick;

I promise, I'll run like the wind,
I'll twist and I'll turn and I'll pass,
I'll dazzle defenders with sparkle and speed,
you won't see my boots touch the grass;

Or maybe, I'll play at the back,
as solid and strong as a wall,
frustrating all forwards who dare to attempt
the slightest approach with the ball;

But—
each time they play, it's the same,
I'm left on the line, in the cold,
they never allow me to join in the game,
they always say,
'Gran, you're too old!'

Rowena Sommerville

Dog Bites Goalie

MICHAEL HARDCASTLE

The dog really didn't look dangerous. Playful was how Steve might have described it.

The first time he noticed the little black-and-white terrier it seemed to be having a game with someone. It kept backing away, backing away and then rushing forward as if being tempted by a prize, a sweet perhaps or a tennis ball. Steve couldn't hear any bark, though, which was unusual with dogs that were getting excited.

Although his team, Rooville, were pinning the opposition in their own half of the pitch at that point Steve daren't risk watching the antics of the dog for too long. But as he patrolled his penalty area he kept shooting glances at it. For some reason he couldn't fathom, it had seized his interest. Even when their goalie brought off a spectacular save and Steve joined in the applause for the skills involved, he still kept an eye on the mongrel.

Then he was distracted by a sudden raid, a solitary striker breaking from the halfway line to try a long-range speculative shot. He'd supposed Steve wasn't concentrating but the Rooville goalkeeper plucked the ball out of the air almost nonchalantly. Afterwards, he remembered showing off a bit by throwing the ball from hand to hand before booting it upfield.

When, moments later, Steve looked round the dog was on the pitch. Worse, it was coming straight for him. Steve thought of giving it a pat but swiftly changed his mind. The dog no longer looked friendly.

'Hey, go on, get off!' he ordered.

Pausing, the dog looked up at him, suspecting something.

'Is it his dog?' Steve heard from someone behind his goal. It sounded like a perfectly natural enquiry. In any case, Rooville's supporters weren't renowned for the quality of their wit.

'Go on, get going!' Steve ordered again when the dog remained motionless. He waved his pink-and-black gloves to encourage a departure.

The dog leapt—leapt and caught its target, its teeth going through the glove like razors.

Pain flared and Steve shook his left hand fiercely. Dog and glove fell away together. Steve's kick was a gut reaction to the injury and the indignity of the attack. It caught the dog under its belly, lifting it high off the ground like a well-struck football. The terrier soared before falling vertically to the turf. It landed without a sound and lay still, stretched out, senseless.

It was the sight of the dog in mid-air that caused the referee to blow his whistle. The referee's first thought (because he caught only a glimpse of the object) was that someone had thrown a missile on to the pitch.

Horrified by what he'd seen, a spectator dashed from behind the goal to tend the animal. Steve, still wringing his damaged hand, was for the moment thinking only of himself. Then, as he watched the spectator, he realized what he'd done. The dog was still motionless as a stone.

His damaged hand thrust into his right armpit in an effort to reduce the pain, Steve, hunched over, went to see for himself. By now another spectator was cradling the animal's head in his arms and urging it to show some life. A middle-aged man in the sort of black cap a foreign seaman might wear looked up as Steve approached.

'Thought your job was to kick the ball, not harmless animals!' he said in a snarl that the terrier might have envied.

'Er, is it your dog?' Steve enquired. His pain was easing a fraction but he wasn't in a mood yet to apologize. In any case, the dog had been the aggressor. It shouldn't have been on the pitch in the first place.

'No, it's not. Don't know whose it is. But it reminds me of that Punch and Judy dog called Toby I used to watch at the seaside as a kid. Always felt sorry for it. Like I feel sorry for this little one after what you did to him.'

By now, most of the rest of the players, the referee and one of the linesmen had gathered round to offer advice or sympathy. Some were not doing much to conceal their amusement. Rooville's coach was rather late in joining them and didn't seem to realize that his goalie really was wounded. His eyes were only for the stricken terrier.

'Look,' said the ref in a reasonable tone, 'I'm sorry about this but you'll have to get this dog off the pitch. You're right on the penalty spot, you know.'

'I'll give you a hand,' volunteered Terry, Rooville's coach. 'When we get over to my kit we'll try the magic sponge on him. Works on most of my players, I can tell you, unless they've broken a leg or something like that.'

'But what about *me*?' demanded Steve, catching hold of Terry.

'This dog's in a bad way because of you,' Terry hissed in reply. 'First things first, you know my priorities.'

'But—' Steve was protesting when the referee touched him on the arm and said that he should return between his posts without delay so that the match could be resumed.

Steve was in a dilemma. Rooville were only a goal ahead in this League Cup Final so if he went off for treatment Pine Valley Raiders would throw everything at them, encouraged immensely by facing only a makeshift goalie. Steve knew that none of his team-mates was really capable of taking his place in goal. All the same, he feared the dog's teeth had caused real damage and he needed professional attention. He hadn't dared take off his inner glove to inspect the wound. His undoubted bravery on the pitch didn't extend to examining his own or anyone else's bloody wounds.

It was wholly predictable that with Rooville's concentration broken, Pine Valley should launch a fierce attack the moment they had possession. Their Number 7, displaying previously unseen wizardry on the wing, sent over a looping centre that Steve would have caught and held nine times out of ten. This time he caught it, couldn't hold it under pressure, and dropped to his knees to scramble for it again in very undignified fashion among hacking boots. He suffered another blaze of pain when someone trod on the already injured hand.

This time courage wasn't enough. He needed urgent treatment, as the ref realized, but Terry was nowhere to be seen so it was Pine Valley's physio who came to his aid. 'Treatment room immediately,' he ordered. 'So don't try and be the hero by staying on. This is for your own good, son.'

The rest of the Rooville players weren't sure this wasn't a fiendish move on the part of the opposition to deprive them of the most vital member of their defence; but they didn't protest. They'd seen the expression on the face of their skipper, Martin, when *he* had seen Steve's hand.

Before that moment Martin had thought he might become the stand-in goalie himself but now he ordered

Darren to put on Steve's black-and-yellow jersey. Darren was a hard man in any situation so he'd be willing to suffer in the cause of a Rooville victory.

'You're lucky this game's being played at a top club ground that has proper facilities for everything,' remarked the physio, his arm round Steve's shoulders as he guided him from the pitch.

Steve didn't see how good luck could possibly come into it: he'd been injured twice, once by a mad dog, and now he was probably out of the Cup Final for good. Most people were never so unlucky in their entire lives. The physio, Ken, had a word with his own bench before leading Steve down the tunnel towards the dressing rooms but Steve was in too much discomfort to worry about what was said.

'We'll get you on the treatment table right away,' Ken told him. 'I've sent for our doctor. Think you'll need some stitches. Oh, and an anti-tetanus jab. Can't be too careful with these sorts of injuries.'

But the treatment table was already occupied. The dog was stretched out on it, full length, being tenderly ministered to by Terry who looked up at them briefly, said, 'Hang on a minute, nearly finished here'—and carried on.

'But I need help,' Steve protested, upset at the presence of the violent black-and-white dog, even if it was still comatose.

Suddenly the dog, possibly alerted by Steve's voice, struggled to sit up and barked fiercely. Steve, thinking it was preparing to fly at him again, backed away.

'Settle down, son, settle down, you're all right,' Terry said, addressing the dog in the same phrase he used to his players. He glanced across at Steve and grinned. 'You do know dogs are our best friends, don't you? So they deserve proper treatment, too.'

'This one's not *my* best friend, I can tell you,' Steve replied sniffily. 'Couldn't be any man's best friend, in my view. He's *lethal* in the goal-mouth.'

'Wish some of our strikers were!' Terry laughed, patting the animal fondly as he completed its treatment. Steve believed it was only because Terry had his hand across its muzzle that the dog wasn't still yapping at him. Steve was sure it looked mad.

'Anyway, perhaps it just doesn't like pink gloves,' Terry went on. 'Can't say I blame it.'

'What?'

'Maybe it thought your pink gloves were tasty meat or something and it just wanted a bit. Dead natural in a dog, that.'

'Well, it's not having my hand again, that's for certain.'

'Anybody know whose dog it is?' enquired Terry, still stroking away. Ken shook his head. 'Well, we could put out an appeal for its owner over the loudspeaker. Can't have just come here on its own— though there are some homeless dogs around, I hear.'

'I heard somebody ask if it was mine,' Steve remarked. 'That's the one real laugh of the day. I'd have it put down if it was mine.'

'Now, now, don't be vindictive,' Terry said soothingly. 'Let's have a look at your wound, son.'

Steve held back. 'Aren't you going to wash your hands after holding that dog? It could have every disease under the sun.'

Terry frowned. 'Look, son, don't tell me how to do my job. I know it a lot better than you do.' All the same, he went across to the sink and washed thoroughly. Ken, who'd been given the dog to hold, now tied it to a drawer handle with a length of twisted bandage. It didn't protest at all but kept its gaze on Steve and its ears laid back.

Rather reluctantly, Steve climbed on to the treatment table, well aware that the dog's eyes never left him. He closed his eyes and submitted to the painful examination of his wounds before the doctor briskly came in, rapidly gave him an injection and then did what had to be done. At least the pain soon disappeared and Steve was able to wonder how long it would be before he could keep goal again. Whatever the outcome of the Cup Final, Rooville had another vital match the following week. As he'd gained his place in the team as a result of another goalkeeper's injury Steve didn't want to lose it for the same reason.

'Only a minute to go and we're still one up,' reported Terry, breaking into his thoughts. 'So you'll probably get a winner's medal, Steve, in spite of missing half the game. Some guys are just *so* lucky.'

Steve gritted his teeth. He couldn't imagine why Terry thought everything had to be a joke. It could only be because he was constantly dealing with other people's pain.

'Right, I think you'll survive, young man,' the doctor told him, indicating that he could get up now. 'Just take things easy and don't try to grab anything, not even a sandwich if you're starving!'

Steve cautiously got to his feet, his glance searching for the dog. It was still there, still watching him, ears still laid back. This time it didn't bark or growl but Steve knew that silence was more ominous than noise sometimes. Terry saw what was happening.

'Come on, you two,' he urged jovially, 'it's time to be best friends. Stupid to be enemies. Look, Steve, just hold out your hand, show there's nothing in it. I'm sure Bonzo will lick it this time. He's used to you now.'

'No way!' Steve retorted. 'I'm risking nothing with that, that killer!'

At that moment there was a subdued sound of cheering and they all knew then that Rooville had won the Cup. The excitement in the treatment room aroused the dog and when Steve moved towards the door, which meant passing in front of the dog, it made a sudden dart at him. Hastily, Steve stepped aside, although this time he restrained himself from kicking the creature.

'See, I told you,' he pointed out to Terry, Ken, and the doctor. 'He'd've bitten me again if I hadn't got out of his way.'

'Oh, well, I reckon he must be allergic to you,' Terry smiled. 'Pity, because if his owner doesn't come for him, we might be stuck with him for good.'

They were. In spite of further announcements to the crowd, the terrier's owner didn't come forward. He'd either decided to abandon him or feared the consequences of possessing a dog that publicly savaged an innocent goalkeeper (which was how Steve described the attack). The team couldn't just leave it at the City Ground and nobody, Steve apart, was prepared to take it along to the Lost Dogs' Home and leave it there.

'Too heartless by miles!' insisted Terry, to general sympathy from the rest of the team, and so it was he who gave it a home with his own family and their many animals.

Martin, who revelled in getting publicity for Rooville at any time, wanted to give the story of the homeless dog to a friendly reporter but Steve managed to stifle that idea. 'They'll make a joke about it, about how the rotten dog bit off more than it could chew, or something like that,' he pointed out. 'They'll say I dropped it or it was a goalkeeping error or *anything* that pokes fun at me, us. Don't do it, skipper, for my sake—the *team's* sake.' So, reluctantly, Martin put the phone down.

They called him Toby because some of the players remembered the sympathetic spectator's references to the Punch and Judy dog. Terry brought him to training sessions. Naturally, Steve steered clear of him and Terry was thoughtful enough to keep the terrier away from his goalkeeper, explaining to the rest of the squad that Steve was definitely 'allergic' to dogs. The players thought that was hilarious and for much of the next hour they produced barks and snarls whenever they were close to Steve; and when he handled the ball they jumped up at him, yapping or snapping their jaws. But, like every other running joke in football teams, they eventually wearied of it and training resumed its normal pattern. With the solitary exception of Steve the players quite took to Toby: they thought, as Darren put it, he was quite 'a spunky dog, scared of nothing, not even big goalies waving pink gloves at him!'

'Well, he brought us luck, no doubt about it,' Martin said. 'As soon as Toby came on the scene, we won the Cup—even won it with a substitute goalie! So he must be on our side.'

'But the dog was the *cause* of us having to use a sub,' replied Steve, hurt that no one remembered that. 'He almost *lost* us the Cup.'

He found he was talking to himself. Everyone else was full of praise for the sharp-toothed terrier and when Darren declared, 'Toby ought to be our official mascot,' the response was enthusiastic. Nobody took any notice of Steve's glum expression.

Suggestions for parading him at matches and providing him with special collars and a jacket advertising Rooville FC were bandied about; and Terry, as Toby's official minder, was listened to with exaggerated respect. Steve knew that he wasn't going to be able to escape the tigerish terrier. He glanced in Toby's direction and wasn't surprised to see the dog's ears flatten and his jaw quiver. There were some situations in life where you simply couldn't win.

Toby was introduced to the crowd at Rooville's next home match and drew a smattering of applause. Encouraged by this reception, Terry decided to take him on a circular trip, leading him on a leash round the ground, stopping now and again for the dog to receive friendly pats. It was only when they passed behind Steve's goal that there was a problem. Apprehensively, Steve turned to watch their progress, was spotted (or scented or sensed) by Toby, who then snarled fiercely and tugged desperately at his leash. The spectators behind the goal laughed when Terry jovially explained that the dog was allergic to their goalkeeper, and that Steve seemed just as strong in his dislike 'of this brave little chap!' Because he was keeping a wary eye on the animal Steve almost let in a goal, saving a speculative shot only through the alarmed call of a full-back and his own swift reflexes.

'Er, I'll move on a bit,' Terry said hastily. But before he'd even reached the corner flag Steve, struck by a sudden idea, was calling him back. Reluctantly, and fearing further insults directed at Toby, the Rooville coach returned.

'Listen,' Steve whispered urgently, keeping one eye on the firmly leashed terrier, 'why don't you station yourself behind the *other* goal? Tiger-teeth here just might fancy going for their goalie. Maybe it's *all* goalies, not just me, that he hates. I mean, some dogs can't stand postmen, so maybe this one feels the same about us. Maybe he doesn't like seeing men in gloves. Could be something as daft as that. So . . . '

Terry nodded in wise-man fashion. 'You could have something there, Steve. I can tell you've been giving this bite business some serious thought. Anyway, good thinking. We'll see what happens.'

Steve noted that man and mascot moved at a brisker pace to reach the other end of the pitch. He wondered how Tegworth Rovers' goalkeeper would enjoy the experience that so soon might await him; and he found that when he took his gloves off to exercise his fingers he couldn't stop himself from crossing them. His wound was healing well but he didn't examine it.

Things happened very quickly after that. Moments after reaching the other end Toby, apparently excited by the goalkeeper's antics, started barking very loudly indeed. The goalie, irritated by the noise, turned to try to silence the dog, still, of course, firmly leashed by Terry.

Rooville's skipper, seeing his opponent so completely distracted, fired in a shot from midfield—and saw the ball sail into the unprotected net.

It had worked even better than Steve hoped. Toby had done his worst (well, not exactly his *worst*) brilliantly. As Rooville celebrated, the distraught goalkeeper yelled insults at Toby and even aimed a distant kick at him. By now, though, Terry was hurriedly walking the dog away from the trouble spot. A spectator and Rooville fan, amused by the whole thing, called out to the goalie, 'Given a chance that little mutt'd bite your leg off. You want to be thankful all he did was bark.'

As it turned out, the local newspaper reporter overheard that remark and was sharp enough to include it in his report of the match which Rooville won by that single goal. And the sub-editor, delighted to be able to put up a different headline, billed the story: 'Dog puts bite into Rooville's attack.'

Steve, no longer Toby's only victim, enjoyed that story as much as anyone.

The Ghosts of Park Avenue

Between the terraces the grasses blow
and nod the setting sun from head to head.
This is a place with nowhere else to go.
As people switch the TV on and settle down
and shadows lengthen from the houses round about,
you listen and you almost hear a shout, a thud,
the hush as the cross hangs, and the long
outrush of a moan as the shot dies, wide again.

Against the barriers the sycamores and elders
sway, shoulder to shoulder. The play
of the wind swings. They are rooted to their spot:
they know they must stay to the bitter end.
This is a place where time has begun
to turn in on itself, to find only the memory
of Saturdays, of afternoons where no one scored
and the bored crowd heckled and sang
for the sake of it, and shuffled home to a kettle
and the classifieds, and game-shows where
at least somebody just like them could win.

Now, when the stanchions and the roofs have gone,
only the steps and low brick walls remain.
The nights come washing over them, and the moon,
white as a floodlight, rises and spreads
its monochrome—and from the tunnel
in twin rows, the teams, running, their shorts
flapping like washday, silently.
And the terrace, silently, responds: the roar
of fifteen thousand hopeful souls.
These are not men but legends that will fade
as dreams do at morning. Till then,
they weave the tall grass with their artistry,
and someone, somewhere in his deepest sleep,
picks up a pass, and sensing glory, twists
and jinks past the back and heads for goal.

Stuart Henson

Mid-Field Haiku

Under the floodlights
on crossed swords of their shadows,
Scottish footballers

Saturday evenings,
lip-reading all the swear words
on *Match of the Day*

Matt Simpson

Pass the Ball, Grandad

DEBBIE WHITE

Every Friday after school, Tommy went to Grandad's house for tea.

Take-away fish and chips with extra-hot curry sauce. Brilliant.

Then, after they'd eaten, Grandad would get out his scrap album. He liked to talk about the old days.

'You wouldn't believe it now, Tom, but I was a champion footballer. Nearly got picked for England once.'

'Did you, Grandad?' Tommy would say. 'Tell me what happened.'

Tommy never tired of listening, even though he'd heard it all before. It was great. Just the two of them.

But on Saturdays, things were different. Tommy got really embarrassed by his grandad then.

He hated the way Grandad would turn up at school football matches wearing his old team kit.

Shirt, socks, boots. Worst of all, those awful, long white shorts. Yuk. Tommy hated seeing Grandad's skinny, purple-veined legs sticking out. They looked horrible.

'Can't you make him stop?' Tommy asked his mum.

She was folding up his goalie kit for that afternoon's match.

'Tom, love,' said his mum, 'you should be grateful he's not *your* dad. When I was your age, Grandad used to meet me and your Auntie Ruth out of school.

'Then he'd make us dribble a football all the way home. A mile and a half of sheer torment. I still get wobbly legs just thinking about it.'

'I wouldn't mind that,' said Tommy. 'It would be great. Can I dribble a football all the way home on Monday?'

But his mum wasn't listening. She was miles away.

'Ooooh,' she shuddered. 'And there was this little squirt called Trevor Davies. He used to follow us, shouting out rude rhymes.'

'What sort of rude rhymes?' asked Tommy.

'I can't remember now. It was a long time ago. Something about droopy knickers, I think.'

What was rude about droopy knickers? he wondered.

Then he said, 'Our new team coach is called Trevor Davies.'

'Is he thin as a whippet?' asked Mum. 'Does he have a ginger crew-cut and eyes like fried eggs?'

'Yes!' said Tommy. 'How did you know? And his nephew Mike Davies is going to be our striker. It's not fair.'

'Is Mike a good player?' asked his mum.

Tommy was torn for a split-second. But he wanted to be truthful, so he sighed and said, 'Yes. He is. He's brilliant. Mr Davies says that one day soon, he's going to be spotted by a talent scout. Then one of the big clubs will whisk him away. He'll be rich and famous.'

An idea struck him. 'If Grandad was playing football now, do you think *he'd* be famous?'

'Maybe,' said Tommy's mum. 'But right now you've a match to play. So here's your stuff. Don't forget to put your muddy boots in the plastic bag. Oh, and it's raining, so I'll drop you off at school. Grandad will be at the match. He'll bring you home afterwards. All right?'

Blazing bananas, thought Tommy. No it wasn't. But Grandad loved to see him play.

By the time they got to school, the rain had turned to a fine drizzle.

'Do you think they'll cancel the game?' asked Tommy's mum.

'No chance,' said Tommy. 'Mr Davies said that even snow wouldn't stop it. It's a dead important match. Forest Hill Juniors hammered us last time. Eight–nil. It was terrible.

'We can't lose this one or we'll be out of the League Cup.'

'Oh, right. THAT important,' said his mum, ruffling his hair. She was about to give him a kiss, but he managed to duck just in time. Saved that embarrassment anyway.

But, oh no! There was Grandad jogging towards them. He had a football under one arm.

'All right, our Tom?' he said. 'Get changed and we'll have a warm up.'

'Grandad,' growled Tommy, trying to look fierce. 'Everyone's looking.'

'Take no notice,' said Grandad. He was touching his toes, wiggling his shoulders, doing side bends. 'They're only jealous!'

'After all,' he went on. 'Not many lads have a grandad who nearly played for England. And don't forget that bit of advice I gave you.

'All good goalies watch the striker's eyes. Where a player's looking, is where he's kicking. OK?'

Tommy sighed. 'Yes, Grandad.' Then he sloped off to join the rest of the team.

As he got closer, he could see Mike laughing and pointing at him.

'Your grandad hoping to join the team?' sneered Mike.

Tommy scowled.

'You leave my grandad alone. He used to be a brilliant player.'

'Oh, yeah?' snorted Mike. 'Who'd he play for then? Tyrannosaurus Rovers . . . or was it Diplodocus Hotspurs?'

'I suppose you think that's funny!' hissed Tommy.

'We do, lads, don't we?' said Mike. He turned to Tommy's team mates. Some of them sniggered.

'Now then. Stop that,' said Mr Davies stepping in quickly to calm things down. But he couldn't help smirking to himself . . . 'Tyrannosaurus Rovers? Ho, ho, ho. Brilliant.'

Tommy glared at Mike and Mr Davies. He felt all hot and angry. Then he remembered what his mum had said about Mr Davies. 'A little squirt with eyes like fried eggs.'

That made Tommy feel better. Anyway, by then the ref had come on to the pitch.

He called the team captains together. They tossed a coin to see who'd kick off. Forest Hill won. They decided to kick into the wind.

Tommy took up his position in goal. He joggled on the spot to keep warm.

He tried to catch the eye of Forest Hill's striker. He was too far away.

Instead he spotted his grandad standing on the sidelines.

He was talking to a short man wearing a smart raincoat. Tommy didn't know who he was, but he was smiling and shaking Grandad's hand.

Then Grandad pointed to Tommy and waved. He waved back.

Tommy was soon too busy with the game to wonder who the stranger was. Forest Hill were on form and playing to win. In the first fifteen minutes, Tommy had to make four saves!

Then it was save number five. Tommy remembered

what Grandad had told him: watch the striker's eyes. See where they're looking.

Yes! Tommy dived to the right. His feet left the ground. His fingers reached out to catch the ball.

He had it safe, even though he'd cracked his elbow on the ground and was covered in mud.

Thanks, Grandad, he thought. Great advice!

Tommy felt good . . . but not for long.

He didn't see what happened, but 'Double-Decker' Dolan was suddenly rolling on the ground. He was clutching his leg.

'Double-Decker' was built like a bus. He was also one of their best players *and* Tommy's second-best mate.

Mr Davies ran on to the pitch. He seemed to be arguing with the ref.

His voice had gone all high and squeaky. He was jabbing his finger right under the ref's nose. But it did no good.

Double-Decker was carried off the pitch with a sprained ankle. Tommy's best mate, 'Worm' Wigley ran on to substitute.

The ref blew his whistle and the match began again.

Mike was playing really well. Tommy had to admit it. His ball control was so good, it made you want to cry.

He wasn't the only one to notice Mike. The man in the smart raincoat had too. Every time Mike had the ball, he'd write in his notebook.

But then Mike got too confident. He started showing off. He was running backwards shouting: 'To me. To me.'

He didn't see Worm Wigley right behind him.

They fell in a tangle of arms and elbows. The ref ran up to see what was going on.

'I think I've broken my arm,' wailed Mike.

'It's all right for you,' moaned Worm thickly. 'I think I've broken my nose. It's bleeding.'

'I'll give you "broken arm and broken nose",' screeched Mr Davies.

He ran over to where they lay in a heap.

'You need your heads banging together. You're a pair of great wet jellies. You've ruined everything. You see that man over there?'

Twenty-two heads turned to where Mr Davies was pointing. But the man in the smart raincoat had turned away. He was shaking his head.

'He's the scout for the local League Club. I've been wanting him to look at Mike for weeks. Now he's going away.'

Mike started crying. Then he tried to stand up. 'I can play with a broken arm,' he snivelled. 'No problem.'

'Of course you can't. Suppose you were tackled. You'd end up breaking something else and then what would your mum and dad say?' Mr Davies was looking harassed.

Mike started crying again. 'Why do I have to play with such a load of idiots?'

'That's not fair!' said Tommy. 'It wasn't anybody's fault.'

'You're right there, son,' said Grandad. He'd come over to see if he could help.

'Just keep your nose out,' said Mr Davies.

'Well, Trevor,' said Grandad. 'I see you're just as rude as ever.'

Mr Davies sniffed and turned to Worm.

'And what about you, Worm . . . I mean William? Think you can still play?' he asked.

But by then, Worm's mum, Patsy, had run over. She was shouting at Mr Davies.

'Don't you speak to my William like that! Of course he can't play. I'm taking him down to the hospital. Come along, William . . . and don't drip blood in the car.'

'Now what?' said Mr Davies, looking over to the side of the pitch.

But there was only Paul Peakle, who never wanted to play. He looked as limp as a piece of wet lettuce.

'Jumping Jehosophat!' Mr Davies looked up at the sky. 'Just my luck.'

Then Tommy saw his grandad tap Mr Davies on the shoulder.

Oh no! thought Tommy. What's he going to say?

'All right, Trevor?' asked Grandad. 'What's the problem?'

'Nothing I can't handle,' said Mr Davies, trying to look as tall as possible.

'One lad short of a full team are you?' asked Grandad, with a lightning grip on the situation.

'Well . . . ' Mr Davies began.

'Are you or not?'

'Yes I am,' said Mr Davies, looking as if someone had just popped his balloon.

'Let me play,' said Grandad.

'You must be joking,' said Mr Davies.

'Let me play,' said Grandad, 'and I'll have a word with the talent scout in the smart raincoat. He's still a big fan of mine.'

Mr Davies looked amazed. His mouth fell open.

'Right,' said Grandad. 'That's settled. But first we'd better get Mike seen to. Looks like he's in pain.'

'Thanks,' whispered Mike. 'Tommy's lucky to have you as a grandad.'

'You're right there!' said Grandad, smiling. 'Now where do you lads keep the spare kit?'

Tommy could have died. There was Grandad squeezed into the Junior School strip.

His legs looked worse than ever. As for the shirt, it barely reached across his shoulders.

'Now just hold on there,' said the ref, coming across

to Grandad and Mr Davies. 'He can't play. He's a grown-up.'

If only, thought Tommy.

'I'm past being one of those,' said Grandad. 'I'm over the hill and going fast down the other side. I'll be seventy next month.'

'Oh, go on then . . . ' said the ref. He blew his whistle.

'Let me at 'em,' said Grandad.

Tommy couldn't believe his eyes. His grandad was really good. In fact, he was brilliant.

Ducking and diving, dodging and weaving. His ball control was still masterly. At half-time, the score was one–all.

Not bad. But Tommy could see Mr Davies was worried. He was chewing his scarf.

Then Tommy got the ball. He looked around. What should he do? He saw Grandad down the field.

He kicked the ball straight to Grandad's feet.

With only a minute to go, Grandad saw his chance. But then he came up against Forest Hill's sweeper. She towered over him.

Terri 'Queen of the Foul' Taylor went to tackle. But she didn't go for the ball.

Instead she caught Grandad behind the knee with her boot.

He was rolling on the floor, holding his knee. It was just outside the penalty area.

'She whipped me legs out from under me, ref,' cried Grandad.

'I never!' yelled Terri. But no one believed her.

The ref blew his whistle. 'Free kick!'

He'll never be able to take that, thought Tommy.

But Grandad leapt to his feet and placed the ball with care.

Seven of the Forest Hill team had made a wall in front of their goal. No one could get through that . . . or could they?

Their goalie was standing on the left. So Grandad kicked the ball with the outside of his foot.

It was a great shot. It swerved over Forest Hill's defenders. Bang! Straight into the top right-hand corner of the goal.

It was the last kick of the game: 2–1.

Grandad was a hero. The team even tried to carry him off the pitch, but he was too heavy.

They had to make do with slapping his back and shouting, 'Come on, you Grandad.'

'Well done,' said Mr Davies, pumping Grandad's arm up and down till his head wobbled. 'I never knew you were so good.'

'I'm dead proud, Grandad,' said Tommy. And he was.

'There's life in the old dog yet,' said Grandad.

'Can we dribble your football all the way home then?' said Tommy.

'Certainly,' said Grandad and he set off.

'I'll be here next week,' he said to Mr Davies as he passed. 'If you need me.'

Unfair

When we went over the park
Sunday mornings
To play football
we picked up sides.

Lizzie was our striker
because she had the best shot.

When the teachers
chose the school team
Marshy was our striker.

Lizzie wasn't allowed to play,
they said.

So she watched us lose, instead . . .

Michael Rosen

Making a Meal of It

What did you do at school today?
Played football.
Where are you going now?
To play football.
What time will you be back?
After football.

Football! Football! Football!
That's all I ever hear.
Well!
Well don't be late for tea.
OK.

We're having football casserole.
Eh?
Followed by football crumble.
What?

Washed down with a . . .
As if I can't guess!
nice pot of . . .
I'm not listening!
  . . . tea.

Bernard Young

You Tell Me

Here are the football results:
League Division Fun
Manchester United won, Manchester City lost,
Crystal Palace 2, Buckingham Palace 1
Millwall Leeds nowhere
Wolves 8 A cheese roll and had a cup of tea 2
Aldershot 3 Buffalo Bill shot 2
Evertonill, Liverpool's not very well either
Newcastle's Heaven Sunderland's a very nice place 2
Ipswich one? You tell me.

Michael Rosen

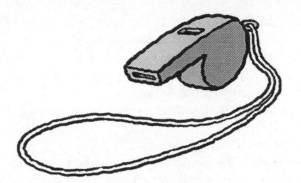

The Big Match

ROB CHILDS

'Is it never going to stop?' Chris whined.

The two boys stared miserably out of their rain-spattered bedroom window.

'It's been raining for hours,' Andrew muttered. 'The match will be called off at this rate.'

Chris was appalled.

'Off! You mean, cancelled?'

His dreams began to disappear down the drain with all the rainwater.

'Could be. Pitch waterlogged, they call it.'

'It can't be!' Chris cried out. 'Simon'll be fit again then before I even get a chance to play.'

They looked at each other with equal dismay.

'C'mon, it'll probably be OK,' said Andrew more optimistically. 'No use worrying about it. Let's try and get some sleep.'

They lay in the darkened room, Chris too tense and nervous to close his eyes as he thought about Andrew's final words before he had switched off the light. 'If we do play tomorrow, it's sure going to be muddy. We'll be sliding about all over the place. Great!'

But the likelihood of a slippery ball to handle was not helping Chris's peace of mind at all.

Suddenly he sat bolt upright in bed.

'Gloves!' he exclaimed loudly. 'Oh no! My goalie's gloves. I've left them at school.'

'You idiot!' came a weary reply from nearby. 'You're hopeless.'

'What can I do?'

'Nothing. They won't go and open up the school just for you, so you'll just have to manage without. Serves you right—it might improve your memory in future.'

Slowly, however, even the sleepy Andrew began to appreciate the possible serious consequences for the team. 'Haven't you got any others to wear?'

Chris shook his head. 'Only my ordinary gloves. Mum would go mad if I messed them up.'

They considered the problem for several minutes until Chris let out a whoop.

'The witch's gloves!'

He scrambled out of bed and fished them out from the top drawer of his cabinet.

'I thought you'd already taken them into school for the jumble,' Andrew said.

'I kept forgetting,' Chris confessed, and then laughed. 'You see, it helps to have a bad memory sometimes!'

Andrew gave up and watched his brother pull them on.

'They're nice and rough so I'll be able to grip the ball OK, I reckon. Good old witchy! Hey! They might even have a lucky magic spell on them.'

'Fat chance of that,' Andrew scoffed. 'More likely to be unlucky, if you ask me. But I suppose they're better than nothing. How do they feel?'

'Ace! They fit like a glove!' Chris joked.

Andrew collapsed back on to his pillow with a groan

164

and then decided to throw it at him to stop him prancing around the room.

After heavy overnight rain, the new day dawned grey and chilly, but a strong, gusty wind was helping to dry out some of the puddles of water lying in every hollow. The brothers ran all the way to the ground, desperate to find out whether the big match was still on or not, and arrived breathless to join a few others already there.

'Lovely and squelchy!' They heard Duggan's voice raised above the rest. 'Little Westy is going to be a real stick in the mud today.'

He was standing in the goalmouth as they approached, the mud oozing over the toes of his wellingtons. There were a few pools of brown water to be seen in the centre circle and both penalty areas, but the state of the pitch down the wings did not seem too bad.

'What do you reckon?' Andrew asked Tim Lawrence, who would have to plough through the mess in midfield more than most.

'Mr Jones told me he thought it was playable if there's no more rain,' Tim replied, 'but the final decision's up to the referee. He's inspecting the pitch now.'

'Are Shenby here yet?' Chris asked.

'Not yet,' Duggan interrupted quickly. 'Getting cold feet, are we?

'No. Just wondered, that's all,' he defended himself.

Even so, he could feel the butterflies churning around inside his stomach with his hurried breakfast. He hated standing about waiting, and he was impatient for things to start happening.

At that moment Mr Jones came across to them. He tried to look as though he had bad news but couldn't keep his face straight as he saw the disappointment in their eyes. 'It's OK, lads,' he grinned at last, 'we're going ahead and hoping for the best.'

They let out a cheer of relief and he had to calm them down again before he could continue. 'It's bound to be tricky underfoot so keep it simple. No fancy stuff near your own goal in this mud. Get the ball away to safety.'

He looked at Chris uneasily. 'Not ideal conditions for your first game, I'm afraid, but good luck. Watch for the ball skidding about. And don't worry, whatever happens, nobody's going to grumble at you if you do make any mistakes.'

Chris shot a glance at the smirking Duggan and felt that this last remark was perhaps not strictly accurate.

'Have you got some gloves?' Mr Jones asked him.

He gulped and avoided Andrew's face. 'Yes,' he said simply.

'Good. You'll certainly be needing them today.'

As he spoke, a convoy of vehicles began to unload a cargo of eager Shenby footballers and Mr Jones went off to welcome them, leaving his own players to troop into the wooden changing hut. Chris felt a gentle nudge on the arm.

'All the best,' whispered Grandad into his ear, and Chris turned in delight. 'Keep your eye on the ball— the wind will be swirling it about this morning.'

'I will, Grandad.'

They grinned at each other and Chris felt reassured, but quickly he was swallowed up inside the noisy, excited atmosphere of the hut, as both teams hurriedly changed.

At last came the moment that he had dreamed of for ages. Mr Jones held out to him the school team goalkeeper's green top with the black figure 1 standing out on the back. The number 1 keeper in the world, he pretended it meant.

'A little earlier than I'd planned,' the headmaster smiled, 'but I'm sure you'll be seeing a lot more of it in time to come.'

The boy clutched his prize lovingly close to his chest as if to prove his dream had indeed come true. 'Thank you,' he murmured.

As soon as he pulled the jersey over his head all nervousness and doubt vanished. He was ready to face anybody. No matter how many more times he might wear it, he knew that he would never forget that first marvellous sensation of feeling its extra padded warmth against his bare skin.

Now he was a real goalkeeper!

He swiftly slipped into his white shorts, tugged on the red socks and laced his boots up tightly. Then, the witch's gloves in one hand, he clattered down the steps out on to the soft, spongy turf. Danebridge's red and white stripes mingled with Shenby's blue shirts as the two sides jogged towards the pitch to warm up. Their bright, freshly-washed kits were not destined to stay those colours for long, however, on such a mud-heap.

The new young goalkeeper spotted his grandad on the touchline giving him an encouraging thumbs-up signal. The importance of the occasion was reflected by the fact that his usual place behind the garden wall was not near enough today to enjoy his grandson's performance to the full. Chris waved back and then returned the greetings from some of his own friends kicking a ball about just off the pitch.

The fleeting thought entered his head that normally he would have been there with them, playing their own little game and only half watching the main action, but still managing to raise a cheer when Danebridge scored a goal. Today, though, was very different. He knew they would have given anything to be able to swap places with him and actually play for the school team.

Chris forced himself to put them out of his mind and to concentrate on the job in hand. He saw that the goalmouth nearer the River Dane was in a far worse state than the other and realized that the wind was blowing towards it too. Not surprisingly, his spirits sagged a little when the Shenby captain won the toss and indicated he wanted to attack that way first in the hope of gaining an early advantage.

'Just my luck,' he muttered to himself.

Tim Lawrence, though, did not seem to mind. 'Suits us,' he called to his team, clapping his hands to urge them to play well. 'We'll have the wind behind us in the second half when they're tiring.'

He managed a quick word with Andrew. 'Keep the defence tight. We've somehow got to hold on till half-time. Try and give Chris an early feel of the ball, if you can, to settle him down.'

The referee blew his whistle and Chris stood alone in the swampy goalmouth as the game at last kicked off, his face set with determination to do well.

But his soccer career was fated to get off to a disastrous start. By the time he did get his hands on the ball, Danebridge were already one goal down in the most tragic manner and there was nothing that he could have done to prevent it.

In Shenby's very first attack, they swept the ball down the right touchline to allow their winger to run at the home side's left-back. Normally the defender would have easily cut out the danger, but as he turned, his feet slithered from underneath him on the greasy surface and his opponent raced past him into the clear.

The winger dribbled into the penalty area and seemed to be trying to set himself up for a shot. Chris was correctly positioned at the near post to block it when, unexpectedly, the ball was hooked hard and low across the face of the goal.

Andrew had been hurtling in to mark their centre-forward and had no chance to get out of the way of the speeding missile. It struck him on the left knee and flew off wickedly into the top corner of his own goal.

The brothers gaped at each other in horror as Shenby celebrated their lucky success. For Chris, it seemed as though time itself stood still. His feet felt so heavy he could not even move them.

Everything, somehow, faded far away and he felt very small and lonely. His dream-world had caved in around him and the prickle of salty tears stung behind his eyes.

Vaguely, a familiar yet strangely pathetic voice got through to him.

'Sorry, little brother,' he heard it apologize. 'I couldn't help it—honest.'

'Forget it, both of you. C'mon, we've got work to do.'

Tim had already fetched the ball and now ruffled Chris's hair to try and cheer him up. 'Nobody's fault,' he continued. 'Let's just get on with the game.'

Similar shouts of encouragement were now floating across from the people on the touchline, but Chris didn't want to look over to where Grandad was standing. He still felt so miserable.

He didn't have much time to gaze around anyway. All too quickly Shenby were threatening his goal again, but this attack broke down and Chris was able to gather up the loose ball and boot it away upfield to get rid of some of his frustration. His first touch had not been a very happy one.

Things almost worsened a minute later when the score nearly became 2–0 after he misjudged a shot completely. He thought he had it covered until the ball dipped in the wind, bounced awkwardly just in front of him and then squirmed through his fingers. With great relief, he saw it swerve to one side and clip the outside of the post instead of going in.

'Good job for you,' came Duggan's angry warning from nearby.

'Leave him alone,' Andrew challenged, 'and let him settle down. He'll be all right. You get back up front and score us a goal.'

'Seems like you're doing all the scoring round here,'

Duggan taunted with a sneer, reminding him painfully of his own goal.

Shenby continued to press hard to try and increase their lead. His confidence shattered, Chris fumbled more shots and the whole defence caught his jitters as they panicked and miskicked their clearances.

Added to these troubles on the pitch, Chris became aware of other irritations behind his goal. A couple of older Shenby boys had wandered up and were now deliberately trying to put him off. Their first casual comments were soon followed by jeers and insults at his mistakes, and then they began to throw little chunks of mud in his direction when they thought no one was looking.

But somebody was.

One piece caught Chris on the back of his neck. 'Pack it up,' he shouted, but that only made them laugh and do it even more. He was at a loss to know how to cope with the situation.

Help arrived, however, before matters got out of hand. Grandad did not normally like to interfere, but today was different. He decided to put a stop to their unfair and unsporting tactics.

'Right! No more of that nonsense, you two,' he announced firmly.

Startled by his sudden appearance on the scene, the boys did not even attempt to run off and they found themselves being escorted round the pitch, without fuss, to be left in the charge of the Shenby teacher.

Grandad slipped Chris a wink on his way back. 'They won't be bothering you again this match.'

Chris nodded gratefully, and it was straight after this that he made his first decent save when he flung himself low to his right to smother a fierce drive.

That made him feel a whole lot better, and the thud of another shot into the front of his muddy green jersey signalled to his team that at last their keeper had found his form and they could breathe more easily. They had survived the crisis.

But there were still some heart-stopping moments inside the Danebridge penalty area, as when one inswinging corner flopped into the goalmouth mud to cause a frantic scramble of legs, boots, arms, and bodies. The ball cannoned about off players for what seemed like an age, and twice Chris blocked point-blank range efforts without being able to hang on to it. Finally, the confusion was ended when Andrew hacked it right off the line to clear the danger.

'Thanks!' cried Chris in the excitement. 'That makes up for earlier.'

His entire kit was filthy wet by now, but he became almost unrecognizable moments later when he landed full-length, face down, in the largest of the puddles. He stood up, still clutching the ball from his save, with his hair, face, and body caked in dark, sticky mud, but grinning widely, his white teeth gleaming through all the dirt. He made a comical sight, but he was loving every minute of being in the thick of the action.

Shenby's pressure paid off, however, with a clever second goal and Chris could do nothing to prevent it. A tricky piece of skill from the left-winger allowed him to jink past two tackles and send an unstoppable shot high over the goalkeeper's head.

In smaller-sized, schoolboy goals it would undoubtedly have sailed over the crossbar as well, but in these it passed comfortably underneath.

There were no nets on the posts and Chris had to recover the ball from the hedge behind, but soon he was smiling again when he watched his opposite number make a similar trip. The visitors' goalkeeper had enjoyed a rather idle first half so far and was caught napping completely by a swift breakaway Danebridge raid seconds before the interval.

It was Tim Lawrence who popped up unmarked in the Shenby area to steer a cross coolly over the line to leave his team only 2–1 down, a well-deserved reward after so much hard work in defence.

Mr Jones was quick to praise everyone at half-time and give them further encouragement. 'The wind's in your favour now in the second half, remember, so go out and show them how to attack.'

He turned to Chris. 'Well played! You've done us proud after a shaky start. But keep on your guard still—it's not over yet.'

It was just as well that Chris did remain alert.

Straight after the re-start the big Shenby centre-forward burst clear for goal with only the keeper to beat. But as he tried to dribble past him, Chris pounced and spread himself down at his feet, grabbing the ball as the attacker sprawled forwards on top of him.

Enjoying the applause, Chris kicked the ball triumphantly away and his brave, important save inspired the whole Danebridge team to put together a series of skilful attacks of their own to prove that they could play good football too.

Even so, it took ten minutes before Shenby cracked, and then they conceded two quick goals.

The equalizer was scored by John Duggan, challenging strongly as usual in a goalmouth scramble and forcing the ball over the line. Immediately afterwards, with Shenby's defence still disorganized, Tim set off on a thrilling solo run, showing superb balance on the slippery ground. Dancing round several tackles, he cut inside from the right and hit a beauty into the far corner beyond the keeper's desperate dive.

Danebridge suddenly found themselves 3–2 ahead and looked well set for victory.

'You've got 'em on the run now,' one of the fathers called from the touchline. 'Keep it up. Let's have more goals.'

But the boys on the pitch knew it was not as simple as that. Shenby were far from finished. They refused to give in, and in fact the shock of falling behind had seemed to put fresh life into them, as they now charged around in search of the equalizer which would earn them a replay at home.

The Cup match became an exciting end-to-end battle as the teams threw everything they had left at each other and both goals survived several narrow squeaks. Time was rapidly running out, though, for Shenby when they forced Chris to tip the ball round the post for yet another corner and Tim signalled everyone back into the penalty area to protect their slender lead.

The winger played a neat short-corner before whipping the ball across into the box through a great ruck of bodies. It suddenly loomed up in front of the unsighted Duggan who reacted by blocking it with his hand in panic before a Shenby player could get at it.

As he booted it away, the Shenby team and their supporters were already loudly demanding a penalty for hand-ball and he slumped to the ground in distress.

'It was an accident, I didn't mean to,' he pleaded, shaking his head and failing to find any excuse for his stunned team-mates. 'I don't know why I did it—it just happened . . . '

The referee had no choice, however, but to award a penalty kick and all their hard work seemed to be wasted. Duggan's eyes were not the only ones to be fixed now on goalkeeper Chris in the desperate hope that he could yet somehow rescue the situation.

John Duggan wished he had not said so many nasty things to him, but it was too late to make up for that now. At least the kid was a good keeper, he had to admit to himself in consolation.

Chris had certainly proved that today to everyone, whatever happened in these next few minutes.

He settled himself on the goal-line, surprised that he felt quite calm considering that everything was at stake and it all seemed to depend upon him. He had never faced a proper penalty like this before and he was not really sure what to expect. The goal around him looked massive and he stared instead at the leather ball, noticing all the dirty marks on it as it sat perched up on the muddy penalty spot a few metres directly in front of him.

The spectators grew hushed in anticipation of the duel, the final shoot-out, and some of the players grouped around the edge of the area hardly dared to watch as the Shenby captain prepared to run in to take the penalty.

Duggan stood, head bowed, hoping for a miracle.

Grandad removed the pipe from his mouth, moistened his lips with his tongue and said a little silent prayer.

Mr Jones wiped his hand nervously down his face as the suspense and tension mounted.

But they could do nothing more to help. It was simply all up to Chris.

He crouched on his toes, waiting. Something Grandad once said about saving penalties suddenly flashed into his head: 'Decide which way to dive and do it—don't be tricked into changing your mind.'

He rubbed his gloved hands together to scrape off some of the mud which clung to them, and then decided: he would go left. Somehow, he had to get in the way of it . . .

The whistle sounded in the silence, and the kicker moved confidently in.

Wham!

The ball was blasted hard and he dived, almost blindly, to his left. But too far!

His hunch had proved correct, but the ball had been struck only just left of centre and he felt it smack against his legs.

Chris lay helpless on the ground as it rebounded off him and the screams from the crowd jerked everybody into action.

Duggan's head shot up to see the stranded keeper

trying unsuccessfully to scramble to his feet in the slime and the penalty-taker flat out too. He had lost his footing as he kicked the ball and was too dazed at his miss to recover quickly enough.

The ball was spinning crazily right in front of the vacant goal, but it was Andrew who reached it a split second ahead of other lunging feet to whack it out of sight.

The whole Danebridge team mobbed the brothers in sheer delight as the cheers rang out from the touchline.

'I take it all back!' shouted Duggan with huge relief. 'Fantastic save, Westy. Simon wouldn't have smelt it!'

'Just lucky,' Chris tried to say modestly, but his new friend wouldn't accept that.

'Don't talk rubbish. It was magic! Thanks for getting me off the hook. I'd never have heard the last of it if they'd scored.'

Chris certainly never heard the last of that save. It was talked about for the rest of the season and beyond.

They would probably have kept talking then if Mr Jones had not managed to get their minds back on the game. But for Shenby it had been a cruel blow. Their heads went down and they could not hide their disappointment. They now seemed resigned to defeat and were fortunate, in fact, not to concede another goal before the final whistle blew shortly afterwards.

The Danebridge players celebrated their passage into the next round of the Cup by exchanging the traditional three cheers with Shenby as they gathered together at the end.

'What a game! What a game!' Andrew kept yelling, as he and John Duggan lifted Chris up on to their shoulders to carry him off the field in honour.

As for Chris, he couldn't quite believe it was all happening to him. It seemed almost unreal. But one thing he was sure about. Magic spell or not, the witch's gloves would never see the jumble sale. He would keep them for himself as a souvenir, a secret reminder of this special day as the school team goalkeeper.

Grandad walked back behind the footballers towards the hut with Mr Jones, enjoying their obvious pleasure.

'Thanks for making a young boy very happy . . . and an old man too,' he said with a chuckle, his eyes wet and shining.

'Not my doing,' the headmaster replied, reflecting the credit back on to Chris. 'He took his big chance with both hands today. He's a hero now. A muddy hero!'

Acknowledgements

Rob Childs: extract from *The Big Match* (Young Corgi, a division of Transworld Publishers Ltd, 1987), © Rob Childs 1987, reprinted by permission of Transworld Publishers Ltd and David Higham Associates Ltd. All rights reserved.

Hannah Cole: 'Away Game' extract from *Kick-Off* (Julia McCrae/Walker Books, 1989), reprinted by permission of David Higham Associates Ltd.

Paul Cookson and **David Harmer:** 'FA Rules OK' from David Orme (ed): *'Ere We Go* (Macmillan, 1993), reprinted by permission of the authors.

Peter Dixon: 'And Here Are the Football Results' from *Over The Moon* (Red Fox, 1996), reprinted by permission of the author.

Pam Gidney: 'A Perfect Match' first published in David Orme (ed): *You'll Never Walk Alone* (Macmillan, 1995), reprinted by permission of the author.

Michael Hardcastle: 'Dog Bites Goalie' from *Dog Bites Goalie and Other Stories*, (Methuen Children's Books, 1993, a division of Reed International Books Ltd), copyright © Michael Hardcastle 1993, reprinted by permission of Reed Books.

Stuart Henson: 'The Ghosts of Park Avenue' from *Over The Moon* (Red Fox, 1996), reprinted by permission of the author.

Barry Hines: extract from *A Kestrel for a Knave* (Michael Joseph, 1968), copyright © Barry Hines 1968, reprinted by permission of Penguin Books Ltd and The Agency (London) Ltd. All rights reserved and enquiries to The Agency (London) Ltd, 24 Pottery Lane, London W11 4LZ.

Sam Jackson: 'The Secret Weapon' from *Quids for Kids—We Are Champions* (Orion, 1997), copyright © Sam Jackson 1997, reprinted by permission of the Jennifer Luithlen Agency on behalf of the author.

Wes Magee: 'Football!' and 'Ms Jones, Football Teacher', copyright © Wes Magee 1996, both from *Over The Moon* (Red Fox, 1996), reprinted by permission of the author.

Bill Naughton: 'The Goalkeeper's Revenge' from *The Goalkeeper's Revenge and Other Stories* (Puffin, 1968), reprinted by permission of Thomas Nelson & Sons Ltd.

Gareth Owen: 'Denis Law' from *Salford Road and Other Poems* (Young Lions, 1988), copyright © Gareth Owen 1988, reprinted by permission of HarperCollins Ltd and the author c/o Rogers, Coleridge & White Ltd; 'Can We Have Our Ball Back, *Please?*' from *The Fox on the Roundabout and Other*

Football Maths
Don Shaw and John Shiels

Football Maths—Green Strip   Levels 2–3
0 19 838223 5

Football Maths—Yellow Strip   Level 3
0 19 838224 3

Football Maths—Red Strip   Level 4
0 19 838225 1

Football Maths—Blue Strip   Levels 4–5
0 19 838226 X

Which league are you in for maths?

What's your record like this season?

Improve your scoring power by tackling these graded mathematical games, and make yourself champion of the class!

Work your way up through these National Curriculum levels, to get a higher score in your maths tests!

Published in association with Bobby Charlton Soccer Schools

Age 7–11

The Young Oxford Book of Supernatural Stories
Dennis Pepper
Hardback and paperback

The Young Oxford Book of Ghost Stories
Dennis Pepper
Paperback

The Young Oxford Book of Nasty Endings
Dennis Pepper
Hardback and paperback

The Young Oxford Book of Aliens
Dennis Pepper
Hardback

The Young Oxford Book of Folk-tales
Kevin Crossley-Holland
Hardback